# NIGHT DIVE!

Hutto double-checked the plane's controls. The automatic pilot was on, the wind at the plane's tail, the heading correct.

He had never liked night dives. They made him feel as if he were leaping into the air like a Mexican cliff diver, blindfolded and drunk, not knowing if he would hit the swell of the wave or the sharp rocks below. And he knew the seventy pounds of cocaine in his pack would make him feel heavier, making the sensation of free-falling seem faster than normal.

Hutto looked down and could see the black sloping mountain tops slowly recede, turning into rounded foothills. Off to the left he could make out the lights of Pigeon Forge.

He took a deep breath and then stepped out of the plane's door into the darkness.

## ESPIONAGE FICTION BY WARREN MURPHY AND MOLLY COCHRAN

GRANDMASTER                    (17-101, $4.50)
There are only two true powers in the world. One is goodness. One is evil. And one man knows them both. He knows the uses of pleasure, the secrets of pain. He understands the deadly forces that grip the world in treachery. He moves like a shadow, a promise of danger, from Moscow to Washington—from Havana to Tibet. In a game that may never be over, he is the grandmaster.

THE HAND OF LAZARUS            (17-100, $4.50)
A grim spectre of death looms over the tiny County Kerry village of Ardath. The savage plague of urban violence has begun to weave its insidious way into the peaceful fabric of Irish country life. The IRA's most mysterious, elusive, and bloodthirsty murderer has chosen Ardath as his hunting ground, the site that will rock the world and plunge the beleaguered island nation into irreversible chaos: the brutal assassination of the Pope.

*Available wherever paperbacks are sold, or order direct from the Publisher. Send cover price plus 50¢ per copy for mailing and handling to Pinnacle Books, Dept.17-264, 475 Park Avenue South, New York, N.Y. 10016. Residents of New York, New Jersey and Pennsylvania must include sales tax. DO NOT SEND CASH.*

# BAILOUT

## CHARLES BLAKE JOHNSON

**PINNACLE BOOKS**
**WINDSOR PUBLISHING CORP.**

PINNACLE BOOKS

are published by

Windsor Publishing Corp.
475 Park Avenue South
New York, NY 10016

Copyright © 1989 by Charles Blake Johnson

All rights reserved. No part of this book may be reproduced in any form or by any means without the prior written consent of the Publisher, excepting brief quotes used in reviews.

First printing: September, 1989

Printed in the United States of America

## Chapter One

They were too low. Hutto could feel it. Since dusk the Cessna 404 had been running without lights, following the Appalachian Mountains northward, barely clearing the round shapes below.

Hutto peered into the darkness, wondering about their chances of surviving this little adventure.

"If we're as low as I think we are, you're going to bounce," he said.

"No way," Wilson said.

Wilson thought he knew everything about airplanes and how to jump out of them. Hutto figured Wilson knew just enough to get them both into big trouble someday, and it looked like that day was today. Tonight. Wilson had insisted on flying the plane all the way across the gulf himself, and then up to Tennessee, ducking under radar. You couldn't tell Wilson anything.

"Looks like we're right on top of those hills," Hutto said.

"Nothing looks right in the dark. Not even a woman," Wilson said.

"I still say we're low."

"The altimeter reads right."

Hutto kept looking at the dark mass beneath them. "You didn't reset it," he said. "Coming out of Colombia, you've got to reset it when you're this far north."

"I reset it. You think I'm a damn idiot or something?"

"If we're too low, that stuff we just dropped exploded all over the ground. Think of that, three hundred million bucks feeding the hills."

"Well, if I did reset it, and reset it again, we're really going to be screwed up," Wilson said.

"You're going to think screwed up when you bounce."

"I ain't going to bounce."

"The hell you say. You weigh what?"

"Two-sixty."

"Six feet tall, two hundred sixty pounds. You ought to bounce big."

"Six-two," Wilson said. "Six-two, two-sixty. All this sitting around, I can't lose weight."

"Less ice cream and beer, you could lose."

"No way."

"Bounce and you won't have to worry about it."

"I bounce, you bounce, too."

"Not me. I weigh one-eighty. Plus seventy pounds of stuff in the pack and another ten pounds of gear, that comes to two-sixty, which you already weigh without your pack and gear. You're going to be way up there. Almost three-fifty."

"If I go, I'm gone," Wilson said. "I'd rather worry

about how to spend all that money."

"It'll spend itself."

All the way north, Wilson had talked about the money. He deliberated between buying an island somewhere in the South Pacific and moving to Copenhagen or Luxemburg, where the young blondes were mad for rich Americans.

The money was considerable. Maybe $300 million down there on the ridges, and another $30 million strapped onto their backs when they jumped.

Hutto always had money. Nothing like this, but it was always there when he needed it. Now, though, this play even had his attention. If it worked, he'd never have to worry about anything again. Except staying alive.

That might get tough.

Hell. A normal person could live ten lifetimes on the money Hutto already had, and here he was, putting it all on the line for more, for some unimaginable, uncountable amount of money. But Hutto wasn't normal.

A normal person would never try this cross. Teasing the Cocaine Cowboys wasn't anybody's idea of fun. Hutto and Wilson had thought about it for years, flying loads from Colombia, making connections, helping out a little where they could. But the Cowboys got crazier by the day. They tried to run their business on a corporate plan, where everyone had a specific job, and did it, or got fired. The ultimate firing involved getting dropped without a parachute over the Caribbean from a plane flying at 5,000 feet.

This particular run started like all the others. The plane—brand-new, fast, and big—had come from Orlando. Three different nonexistent corporations bought it from each other in three days. Wilson and Hutto flew it to Fort Myers and sat on the beach a couple of days waiting for orders. Then they flew to a dirt strip in Colombia. The engines blew dust across the field while four men quickly loaded the treasure in the back and refueled the plane.

They flew back toward Florida, keeping low over the water's surface to avoid tracking radar. Once they passed over a yacht with an old guy and four young women. The girls only wore bikini bottoms. They jumped and waved at the plane, laughing, flopping in the warm air.

When the Cessna got over Florida, they rose into normal air traffic lanes and headed north. They were supposed to land at an old airstrip near Crossville, Tennessee, up on the Cumberland Plateau. Some helpers would unload the plane, then Wilson and Hutto would set it on fire, destroying any evidence.

But they had other ideas. It took a month to plan, and Hutto thought it had a decent chance of working if Wilson would just fly the plane right.

Hutto had hiked the Smoky Mountains all his life, so they flew over them rather than the Cumberlands. Along the way, the cocaine shipment was split into five bundles weighing about 140 pounds each. All the kilo packages were rewrapped and taped, then packed into a case. When the plane got into one of Hutto's predetermined positions, a case would go overboard, slowed by a parachute. A homing device beat away inside each case so they could be found without too much trouble.

It sounded like a good plan, but something might foul it up, something like Wilson's stubbornness. There's still time to back out, plenty of time to say no, Hutto told himself. Let Wilson jump, if he wanted to, and then just fly away someplace warm and slow. But the Cowboys would still be after him, he figured, so he might as well make the fight worthwhile. Besides, he hated to quit anything this big.

He'd quit just about everything else that was important, but he'd carry this one through, finish it one way or the other. He'd started life as a rich kid, with a rich daddy and a rich granddaddy, with money rolling in from department stores all over the South. He'd been a hard-hitting high school linebacker, but quit the team for some reason he'd now forgotten. He quit college, too, but not before he made every fraternity party on campus, became the meanest man in all the bars on the strip, and chased women who couldn't be caught.

He left school before they could run him off, saving them the trouble of explaining what happened to his well-heeled folks. The world's biggest party was going on in Vietnam, and he enlisted in the army rather than wait to get drafted. One day he looked around and he was a paratrooper, surrounded by other men who wanted to be the meanest man on earth.

He was strong, fast, and smart, like most of the men in his outfit. He was good in a fight, and in town he told the best jokes, smoked the best dope, and bedded the best women available.

The war held him for two tours of duty. By the end, he'd seen his best buddies killed, and he'd blown apart more human beings than he cared to remember. When he came home, he gave his two silver stars to a stripper in San Francisco.

He went back to college, minded his own business enough to get a law degree, married a cute blonde socialite with magnificent legs, and started to work. The department store business didn't interest him, so he took a position with an old-line Knoxville law firm, and started making a name for himself as a trial lawyer. He bought a big house with a circular drive out front, a string of thoroughbred racehorses he kept on a farm in Kentucky, matching Porsches for his wife and himself, and a beach house at Hilton Head, South Carolina.

Then everything changed when the court appointed him to represent a nineteen-year-old black kid accused of raping a junior marketing major at the university. She'd been at a meeting of her sorority at the Panhellenic Building, and the kid had supposedly encountered her as she walked back to her apartment a few blocks away in Fort Sanders.

After investigating every angle, Hutto was convinced that the kid was innocent. The judge and jury, however, were not. The girl, after all, had positively identified him. Hutto did everything he could. Nothing worked.

He couldn't sleep at night thinking about this kid

spending the best part of his life in prison. Hutto figured he'd failed somewhere. A good lawyer could have gotten the kid off. A good lawyer could have thought of something that would have made a difference.

So Hutto visited his client and arranged for him to break out of prison. He left a gun in the right place when he took the kid to see a psychiatrist, distracted the two guards assigned to them, and saw the client bolt away in his Porsche, which had the keys in the ignition.

A week later the cops caught the kid and killed him in a shootout in a $19-a-night motel in Tifton, Georgia. In court, on trial himself, Hutto couldn't explain why he'd picked that particular time to leave the key in the car, and how his client had known it. He said it was a mystery to him just how that pistol his client waved at the guards had been registered to him. He said he was as surprised as anyone by this. Just a bystander.

Nobody believed him. He spent the next two years in prison. When he got out, his cute blonde socialite wife had taken her magnificent legs elsewhere, and the state bar association denied him the right to practice law.

He had enough money, thanks to daddy and granddaddy, so that he didn't have to work. But a man has to do something with himself, and if he can't work legally, he might as well toil illegally.

That was how he got into the coke-running business. Drink with the wrong people in the wrong places enough, and you get your feet in the door. He used a share of his family fortune to start a flying service. He chartered planes, ferried medical supplies, did any number of legitimate things, but his primary activity was bringing in white powder from South America.

Wilson worked for him, officially, at least. In practice, they were partners. Wilson had been a paratrooper, too. Eighty-second Airborne. Hutto didn't know him in Vietnam, though, which was a good thing, because nearly everyone Hutto had known there was dead.

After a few years of this, Hutto and Wilson decided they agreed on one thing: they both hated the damn Cocaine Cowboys. They'd had enough of them and were going to take them good, just once.

That's why they were doing this, dropping cases several miles apart along the crest of the Smokies. When they finished, they'd fly to Pigeon Forge, a little tourist-trap town nearby. Wilson's girlfriend was waiting there in a Jeep wagon. They'd turn the plane east, toward the Atlantic Ocean, set it on autopilot, then bail out. Night jumps were tough, but they'd both done them before. They could probably make it one more time.

Just to be sure they got out of this with something, they were jumping with all the coke they could safely carry. "If the other stuff disappears, I've still got what's on my back," Hutto had said.

After they hit the ground, they planned to hike back to pick up the cases of cocaine. By then the Cowboys would know something was wrong. But if everything worked right, they wouldn't know where Hutto and Wilson were. The plane should make it to the ocean before running out of gas. It would leave nothing but an oil slick on choppy water.

But nothing would work if Wilson had forgotten to reset the altimeter. The drops would be off, because Hutto had taken the wind into account as he eased the cargo outside. And Wilson, so much heavier than Hutto, would surely bounce. Hutto realized it was possible that he might, too.

"Look," he told Wilson. "Why don't you just climb a couple thousand feet? Then we'll be sure it's okay."

"Why don't you just shut up?" Wilson said. "If we're too high, we'll drift all over hell and back. I don't want to hang up in a tree ten miles from the target."

"Better hike than bounce."

"I tell you, I reset it. I ain't no damn idiot."

Maybe not, but Hutto knew Wilson took unnecessary chances just to see if he could pull them off. He remembered the time Wilson had tussled with Colombian Indians over one of their females, making them late for their takeoff. Then there was the time Wilson broke into the Decatur, Alabama jail to spring a buddy. And there were countless times he'd flown into the heart of storms, made night landings on strange unlighted airstrips, and flown junk planes with single engines and an overload of cargo.

Hutto guessed Wilson could hear himself telling jokes about the time they bailed out at 800 feet with ninety-pound packs. That would go over big with the

Scandinavian girls or the Pacific islanders. Hutto imagined that big throaty laugh of Wilson's as he tossed down another beer and told his story.

Wilson was a fool, but a brave fool. That's the worst kind, Hutto thought. Wilson could fly any kind of aircraft. He was good, a sharp stick man. Nobody could beat him. But sometimes you get too good at what you do, so good the little things, like resetting altimeters, sneak up on you.

Wilson was letting his life get away from him. He's not in control, Hutto thought. Where he'd once been big and strong, he was now big, strong, and fat. Where his mind had been penetrating, the tool of a survivor, it was getting lazy. Too many brain cells killed off by booze, Hutto figured. Wilson had once depended on no one. Now he had a woman, a girlfriend.

"Don't take this wrong, Wilson, but I'm glad this is our last mission together. It's time to quit."

"Man, we've had us some times, huh?"

"Yeah, some times."

"We turned this old world upside down. Ain't never seen nothing like Wilson and Hutto."

"Never."

"We done things nobody could do. We seen things. We been places. Couldn't ask for more, right?"

"Couldn't take any more," Hutto said, and they both laughed.

Hutto looked out his window and saw the black sloping mountain tops slowly recede, turning into more rounded foothills. Off to the left he saw the lights of Pigeon Forge, a plastic town complete with dinosaur putt-putt golf courses, ghost pirate ships, porpoise shows, kiddie water slides, and twangy singing-through-the-nose, down-home country music shows.

## Chapter Two

Wilson stepped out the plane's door first. His body with the bulky pack dropped quickly away into the blackness. Hutto double-checked the plane's controls. The automatic pilot was on, the wind at the plane's tail, the heading correct. It would fly eastward until running out of gas somewhere off North Carolina's Outer Banks, then flop into the sea, just some more ocean garbage.

Hutto took a deep breath, then plunged out the door into the darkness. He had never liked night dives. They made him feel as if he were leaping into the air like a Mexican cliff diver, only blindfolded and drunk, not knowing if he would hit the swell of the wave or the sharp rocks below.

The seventy pounds of cocaine in the pack made him heavier and he had the sensation of free-falling faster than normal, though he thought this couldn't be true, not if Sir Isaac Newton was right. He felt it back there, a wad of dust packed into little bricks, worth more money than a hundred average men would see in a lifetime of labor.

Down below, rising fast to meet him, he saw the lights of Pigeon Forge, mostly white and blue except for the yellow street lamps along the big four-lane highway. After his chute opened he could make out the putt-putt golf courses, the bumper car rides, and the water slides where the kids stood in line all day for a few seconds' thrills. Down there somewhere was an Elvis Presley museum and an old jail made into a car museum, with the car Sheriff Buford Pusser was riding in when he died.

He guided himself toward a softball field, a wide dark spot among the dimmer lights of a residential section. He fought the wind, which wanted to push the parachute eastward into the mountains, and tried not to think of what might be waiting for him on the ground.

Landing hard on center field, he wrapped his chute up quickly, stuffing it away, and looked to see who might have been watching his arrival. He sat on his knees in the outfield grass, keeping a low profile. No cops were parked along the field, smoking cigarettes. No teenagers were in the five rows of bleachers, necking. No insomniacs were strolling down the street. No one was watching, not even Wilson.

Not even Wilson. Then he saw the girl, Wilson's girl, get out of the driver's side of a Jeep wagon, and walk calmly past the backstop and home plate.

Hutto hadn't wanted her here, had tried to figure this operation every way possible to avoid her, but couldn't. Wilson didn't need her, didn't even stop to think about her most of the time, but seemed to think she was crucial to their success.

"Where's Wilson?" Hutto asked, meeting her at second base.

"I think he crashed," she said.

"Crashed?"

"I saw him coming down. The parachute was all strung out behind him, and he went somewhere down that street. I knew you'd be down soon, so I waited for you."

"You're not too shook."

"I'll be shook when this is over."

"I told him he was too heavy."

"He never could listen to anybody," she said.

She watched Hutto reach into the pack and draw out a pistol. He looked at it a moment, then stuck it in the waistband of his pants.

She started for the Jeep. "Hurry your ass up," she said. "Don't you have enough trouble in your pants without that?"

"You haven't seen trouble yet," he said, and took off after her. The cocaine felt like a load of gravel in the pack.

He swung the burden onto the floorboard of the back seat, then slid alongside her in the front. "Let's find him," he said.

"Oh, no," she said. "I couldn't look at him."

"He'll probably come walking out of there mad as a son of a bitch."

"No way he's walking out of there."

"We have to find him."

"What is this, some kind of honor society? You

have to remove your dead from the field of battle?" she said. "Look, he's just a puddle of blood and guts."

"Maybe so. But he's a puddle with a pack worth $15 million to the right people."

"God, you need money that much?"

"It's ours. We beat half the world for this stuff, and I don't want to just give it to some Pigeon Forge cops."

She drove slowly down the street, past the houses with the sleeping owners of the putt-putt golf courses and magic ghost ships and concrete dinosaurs. He looked in all the yards and saw nothing but trees and flowers and plastic deer and bicycles.

"Let's just go," she said. "Let's get out of here."

"We'll find him."

"Fat chance."

"We'll get him. He's here, we'll find him."

"I don't like this," she said.

"What if he's hurt? You'd just leave him?"

"He'd leave me, wouldn't he?"

"I don't know," Hutto said.

"What could we do if he was hurt?"

"Something."

"You'd have to get him to a doctor and you can't do that."

"Well, what if he was hurt and he talked? He could name names and the whole bit."

"Now the truth comes out," she said. "You'd do it, too, wouldn't you? Stick that gun in his ear and away he goes. And you were like a brother, almost."

"We're a pair, ain't we, babe," he said, reaching over to flip a twist of blonde hair behind her ear.

"Don't you touch me," she said.

They rode a half mile before finding him. He was lying on his back in a concrete driveway. His head was out of line with the rest of his body, and his chest stuck up high where the heavy pack had broken his back on impact.

"He's not hurting now," Hutto said. He got ready to run for the body, but then he saw a man just this side of sleep standing by the garage door. A woman in a dressing gown stood by the front steps.

The Jeep slowed at the driveway entrance while Hutto thought about what to do. Then the man spoke, sticking his hands in his jeans pockets. He wore no shirt and his stomach protruded over his waistband. "It's okay," the man said. "We called the ambulance. They ought to have been here by now."

While Hutto thought about this, he heard the siren, and then another behind it. Two sirens on the way, and one almost certainly a cop.

"What happened?" Hutto asked.

"We heard this big ka-thump. Or Betty did. Woke her up. I come out to investigate. We've had a lot of break-ins around here lately. So I looked, and that's when I found him."

"Dead?"

"As a stump."

"Say anything to you?"

"Naw. I think he was dead before he hit the ground. I know my heart would stop, if I was coming down like that."

"Terrible thing," Hutto said.

"Damn fool thing, if you ask me. Jumping out of airplanes at night and all. I mean, I don't know anything about it, but it just seems like damn foolishness to me."

"That's right," Hutto said. "Well, since you've got it under control. I reckon we'll go."

"Hang around and catch the excitement," the man said.

"Thanks anyway."

A couple of blocks further up the street they turned toward the main road, driving slowly. Hutto looked toward the mountains, could see nothing at all, not even their dark shapes. It had been a long night, but there were still hours to go before dawn.

"Well, girl, things are different now," he said.

"Don't call me girl."

"Okay, whatever you are, we're going to have to change plans now."

"Look, smart ass," she started.

"No, you look," Hutto said. "Up to now, you were Wilson's girlfriend, and we needed your help. That's why you were in on this. Now he's gone, and you're taking his place."

"So what?"

"So that makes us partners."

"Partners."

"That's right."

"I don't think I want to be partners."

"You have no choice."

"I'm no commando. I don't know a thing about killing and stealing and all that crap."

"You knew Wilson, right? You know me, right? That's all you need to know. Okay? We can make it work."

"All I know is that right now I just feel like driving straight to Brushy Mountain prison and turning myself in."

"Nobody's going to prison. You can bet on that."

She stopped at the intersection of the main road. "What now?" she asked.

"Turn left," he said, and they headed up into the mountains.

"This is crazy," she said.

"Drive at thirty-five. These cops will be on us if you speed at three in the morning."

"I said, this is crazy."

"Everything I've done is crazy. It doesn't bother me one bit."

"It bothers me."

"This is smart crazy. We pull *this* off and it gets us clean out of all that other craziness."

"You'll never be out of it."

"I'll be clean, and you will, too. We're talking about something in the neighborhood of $300 million. That's $150 million for me and $150 million for you. Pretty good soap."

"I don't know what to do with that kind of money."

"You can buy all the studhosses you can handle and live on the Riviera the rest of your born days, girl."

"Girl," she said.

"Sorry. What are you, anyway?"

"You know my name."

"Elizabeth. Lady Beth."

"Elizabeth is just fine."

"That's right."

"Don't you start, Hutto."

"I'm not starting anything."

"We're partners. All right, I can handle that. Partners. Business associates. And that's all."

"No sweat."

"Hands off, Hutto."

"Hey, have I done a thing? What's wrong with you? Wilson's not dead ten minutes and you're pulling a Miss Priss act on me. Look, we know each other, okay? I know you're no angel. I've seen you flapping around in your nightie and sticking stuff up your nose. This is Hutto you're talking to, not some stranger."

"You're strange enough."

"Look, you must have misunderstood something about me. I'm a gentleman."

"Keep it that way."

"Always," he said. "Always."

The road led out of town, and where Pigeon Forge gave way to the Great Smoky Mountains National Park, the speed limit increased to forty-five. Elizabeth pushed the Jeep up the gradual incline.

"Watch it," Hutto said. "Park cops are the worst."

"You want to drive?"

"Never occurred to me. It's your Jeep. You tired or something?"

"Three in the morning is not my best time."

They drove toward Gatlinburg. The road here split with the Little Pigeon River flowing swiftly over its rocks between the sections of the four-lane. The headlights caught a woodchuck standing like a prairie dog alongside the road. The slopes around them were crowded with rhododendron and oaks and tulip poplars.

Hutto loved these mountains. That's why he hated Pigeon Forge and Gatlinburg so much. Pigeon Forge was at the bottom of his list of awful places. When he grew up, it was a village centered around an old grist mill. Now you could barely find the mill for all the tourist attractions, the Archie Campbell Village, Dolly Parton's Dollywood, the thingamajig that floated you in the air like you were parachuting, and all the kiddie shows. Gatlinburg was next up his list from Pigeon Forge.

As long as he could remember, Gatlinburg had been a tourist attraction. In the old days, it was better, though. Now you could hardly get down the sidewalk for all the portrait painters and the teenagers attending Baptist conventions. The girls would be hanging onto the boys, wearing high school letter jackets, giggling and bouncing along. There was the Santa Claus shop and the pancake restaurants and the dozens of shops selling doodads for sticking atop mantels and in closets, knives that won't cut, moccasins made by Koreans. For an outdoors type like Hutto, Gatlinburg was a place to hurry through on your way to a trail, and a spot to grab a beer on your way back.

Elizabeth steered them into town, past a honky-tonk featuring past-their-prime rock and roll stars, and stopped at a red light where the string of motels began. "What now?" she said.

"Now we wait until the stores open."

"We're going shopping?"

"We have to get you outfitted."

"I don't need a new outfit."

"You need something to make sure you stay in one piece while you pack that coke out with me. The original plan holds, as far as we can make it."

"I'm not sure I can."

"You can," Hutto said. "You will. Otherwise, we are dead ducks. Gone geese."

"I'm not real outdoorsy."

"You want to stay out of Brushy Mountain prison, don't you? Well, now's your time to be Elizabeth of the Mountains. You're going to be a hiker, because we've got no choice."

"What do we do until the stores open?"

"Let's go to the Howard Johnson and eat first. Then we'll think of something."

"That's not exactly my favorite place."

"Anyplace that's open right now is my favorite."

"You'd just park this thing with that load back there?"

"What else are we going to do? If somebody wants it that bad, I guess it's theirs."

"I can't believe we're doing this."

"Don't think about it. Tell yourself we're just going for a hike."

There were six cars in the restaurant parking lot. Hutto figured on two waitresses, a cook, and three customers.

"What do you want me to do?" Elizabeth asked.

Hutto got out of the Jeep. "Lock your doors," he said. "And smile. Smile like you love me. We're a pair now."

He held the door open for her. She made a face at him, then they went inside.

## Chapter Three

"I don't see how you can eat that at this time of day," Elizabeth said. She poked scrambled eggs around her plate, watching Hutto work on a cheeseburger.

"It's fuel. We're going to need strength before this day is done."

"What can be so hard about walking in the woods?"

"With a seventy-pound load?"

"I only weigh 135," she said. "Can't we do it some easier way?"

"I'm thinking on it. I don't know. We had it planned just right, then Wilson goes and punks out on us."

"Let's don't talk about Wilson."

Hutto ate in silence after that. When she couldn't finish her eggs, he cleaned her plate. They left a dollar for the waitress and went to the Jeep.

He told her to pull it around behind the motel and park there, hidden among the guests' cars. "What now?" she asked.

"Don't know about you, but I'm going to sleep. The store won't be open for another three or four hours."

"I can't sleep."

"Suit yourself."

"I mean I can't sleep with you here. I can't sleep around strangers."

"I'm not a stranger."

"I mean I've never slept with you."

"You think everybody's a stranger until you've slept with them?"

"Something like that."

"Maybe we'd better go ahead and get it over with, or you won't be able to sleep at all," he said.

"You'd better stop thinking."

"Suit yourself."

"Couldn't you sleep in the back?"

"The back?"

"Back of the Jeep. Then it'd be like you were in another room."

"Why don't you just count sheep?"

"Won't work," she said.

"Look. We're in a war here, and when you're in a war, you eat all you can eat when you can, and you sleep all you can sleep when you can. Because you don't know when you're going to get another chance."

"Okay. I understand that."

"Good. Good night."

"Well, then, I'll sleep in the back."

"Fine with me."

She let herself in the tailgate and curled up behind the back seat. Hutto concentrated on the stars he could see past the lights and glare. He found Orion and stared intently at it. Orion. A warrior. He made up a two-syllable nonsense mantra and chanted it silently, looking at Orion all the while. It relaxed him, and he put thoughts of Wilson's smashed body aside. Within five minutes he was asleep.

He dreamed about being chased by human beings who turned into bears, who in turn changed into fire. He hopped from the tops of mountains trying to escape and could almost fly. But not quite.

The motel maid woke him up. She stood on the sidewalk near the Jeep, pushing her cart laden with towels, soap, and clean sheets. The cart wheels squeaked, and that brought Hutto awake.

She stopped and watched him straighten up on the seat, stretching. He smiled at her. She smiled back, then went on about her business.

He looked into the back and saw the curled female form. "Wake up," he said.

"I never slept," she answered.

"Thought I heard a snore back there."

"That was your own echo. What time is it?"

"Eight o'clock. The world is stirring."

"I need to go to the bathroom."

So they went back into the restaurant. She ordered coffee, eggs, and bacon. He had another cheeseburger. The first waitress was gone, and Hutto was thankful for that. No use drawing attention to themselves.

"How can you live without coffee?" Elizabeth wanted to know when she got back from the restroom.

"Never could stand it," he said. "I don't even like the way it smells."

"That's weird."

"There's something fundamentally evil about coffee. The way it grabs its victims and won't let go."

"That's even weirder," she said. "Least I don't drink Coke at breakfast."

"Now, Coke at breakfast has pop to it. Zip. It gets you going, and it's friendly. It's not wicked, like coffee."

Breakfast done, they went to the store. It was one of those where you could buy a backpack, an apple, a science fiction thriller, or a pair of dress shoes, spending half again what it would cost in a discount store. But Hutto had no choice.

He picked out a medium-frame pack for her, not the best, but available. The canvas was green, which she didn't like. She preferred blue or red. He insisted.

"Ever heard of camouflage?" he asked.

"It's just so damn ugly," she said.

She wanted a pair of hiking boots, but he made her get a pair of high-topped running shoes. The running shoe companies sensed a lost market among the hikers and had started making versions of their jogging shoes for the trail-stomper trade.

"These are ugly, too," she said.

"You don't have to break them in. The boots would make your feet one big blister in an hour's time. Boots would last longer, but you can make tracks in these shoes *today.*"

He took the pack, shoes, and a plastic water bottle to the counter, grabbed a double handful of peanut butter crackers, M&M's, candy bars, and raisins, and paid the attendant.

Back in the Jeep, they were silent while riding to the Holiday Inn. He went inside, filled their water bottles, and came back grim-faced.

"What's wrong now?" she asked.

"The radio was on with the news. Something about Wilson was on it. Apparently, the whole county is going crazy trying to figure out what he was doing."

"Any news about his partners in crime?"

"Not a word. But they've got to be fools to think he did it alone."

"He could have."

"Not Wilson."

"They don't know that."

"Anybody who knew him would."

"I knew him, and I say he could have pulled it off by himself."

"And I say nobody can pull it off alone."

He motioned for her to drive on. She started the Jeep and headed out of the parking lot, but stopped before reaching the street. "What if I call it quits right now?" she asked.

"What do you mean?"

"What if I want out of this right now?"

"But you're already in it."

"I don't think I want to be in it."

"You should have thought of that a long time ago, before jumping into Wilson's bed."

"Leave Wilson out of it. It's just that I don't feel safe."

"Who does?"

"I mean I'm scared."

"Me, too."

"Really scared."

"You'll be all right."

"Would you let me out of it, if I tried?"

"You're already in it too far."

"See. You'd kill me. You killed Wilson, letting him jump with too much coke in his pack. You'd kill me, too."

"I never killed anybody."

"You lie, too."

"I never killed anybody who counted."

"So I don't count, either."

"I wouldn't kill you. I tell you, I'm not a killer."

"What about in Vietnam?"

"That's different."

"They were people, too."

"That was war."

"You said this is war."

"It is."

"So you'd kill me, too."

"I said I wouldn't."

"I want out," she said. "Keep the damn Jeep and keep your damn old green backpack, too. I want out."

"I can't let you go."

"Well, I can't stay."

"You have to," Hutto said. "Think about your $150 million."

"You can have it. Take my $150 million. Just leave me alone."

"All right, let's put it this way. You go back to Knoxville, and your house will be crawling with cops.

Wilson is a celebrity now. The law, the newspapers, the television stations will want to know every little detail about him. What'll they find in your place? A little coke, a little grass, some pills? Wilson's guns? Let's see. Some grenades, some dynamite, some blasting caps. I think he had a rocket launcher somewhere, too. They'll be calling you a terrorist, and they'll decide you're a menace to society, and they'll lock you away and make you swallow the key. So you can go back to that, or stay with me, and have a pretty good shot at seeing your way through to $150 million."

She slumped against the steering wheel. "Now that you put it that way, where to next?" she said.

"Over there," he said, pointing right. She drove up the road, entering the national park, winding about three miles to the foot of Mount Le Conte. They parked in the lot there, and he helped her into her gear.

His outfit was more complicated. He had a survival knife strapped to one calf and a pistol in each side pocket of his pack. The rear pocket was full of extra ammunition clips. He double-checked everything in the back seat before lifting the load to his shoulders.

"Don't I get a gun?" she asked.

"Weapon. You don't need a weapon. You'd just hurt yourself."

"You've got two. I want one."

"You don't know how to use it," he said, setting off for the Rainbow Falls trail.

"But I need it," she said.

"It's non-negotiable," he said, and left her standing there trying to tighten the waist strap of her pack.

When she caught up, he was standing off the trail alongside a stream rushing down the mountain. A log sawed in half lengthwise stretched across the water.

"What's the deal?" she asked.

"Quiet," he said, and continued staring across to the other side.

After a few silent minutes, he crossed the footbridge, motioning her to follow. In the big scramble of rocks on the other side, out of sight of the main trail, he crouched, listening. She followed and he had to catch her waist to keep her from sliding down the rough rocks.

"What are you doing?" she whispered.

"Getting rid of this," he said, pointing at the pack. "Wait here."

Then he walked — calmly, like any hiker might through a glade filled with ferns, rotting leaves, and moss — to a big white oak that looked mostly dead. Once there, he took the pack off, leaned it against the tree, and fiddled with it a while, as though he were adjusting the straps. When nothing else disturbed the quiet, he opened the top flap and quickly removed the brown packages inside, placing them in the hollow section of the tree.

When he got back to the rock pile, he said, "If something happens to me, go to that tree. That's our bank."

"Why didn't you just leave it in the Jeep."

"Didn't you read the Park Service sign? Fifty break-ins in this parking lot in the past year. The Park Service guys are too busy out impressing the tourists to patrol the trail parking lots. They'd rather give directions to young ladies wearing short-shorts than sit around here catching vandals."

"It's safer in the tree, then?"

"By a long shot. Nobody's going to be looking in that tree. Maybe a bear, and I'm not scared of any bear, not black ones like we have around here, anyway."

They recrossed the stream and headed up the trail.

"How far?" she asked.

"Six miles to the top, more or less, and the stuff could have come down a ways from there."

"God, I'll never make it."

"This is just the start, girl."

"Girl."

"Sorry."

"How many of these things are there?"

"More than we'll need."

"That doesn't answer my question."

"Five."

"Just five?"

"Nice round number, isn't it?"

"We'll never find them."

"Hey, you're not off in the woods with a dummy. I'm tracking them."

"What are you talking about?"

He reached back into a side pocket of his pack and pulled out a little box with a red button and several switches.

"What's that?"

"My Klecko," he said. "Best tracking device made."

"I don't get it."

"Each package went down with a homing device

inside. It'll put out silent beeps that this Klecko can pick up. All we have to do is follow the Klecko, and we'll find them. Simple."

"I still don't understand why you couldn't just land and unload the stuff, like any sane person would do."

"A sane person wouldn't do this," he said.

"You're telling me."

"Speaking of which, how much did Wilson tell you about this little caper?"

"All he said was to meet him at the softball field in Pigeon Forge. He said you two would tell me what to do after that."

"You fell for that?"

"I guess."

"So you don't understand any of this?"

"No."

"Sweet Jesus. That Wilson, he was a sweetie pie, huh?"

"I thought we weren't going to talk about him."

"Here's the part he didn't tell you. You knew we were in the drug business, right? That's what paid for the sports cars and bar tabs and the fancy toys. Okay, so we got tired of taking all the risks for a bunch of weirdo Colombians who didn't do a thing but got most of the money. If we got caught on a run, those guys could care less. But if we screwed up, it's our necks. So Wilson and I went to Colombia, picked up a full load of coke in our Cessna, flew up here and threw it out the back in five loads. We tried to drop them close to the Appalachian Trail so we could get to them without too much trouble. Then we flew to Pigeon Forge, set the plane on automatic pilot so it'd fall into the ocean and disappear, and jumped out to meet you. We carried some coke with us, just to be sure we wound up with something in case everything went haywire. That's where you came in. You were going to drive the Jeep and meet us while we hiked up and brought the coke down. We were going to get one or two a day, spend the night in motels, then drive it out and sell it to the Italians, who hate the Colombians."

"You mean the Mafia is in on this, too?"

"That's the way the script reads."

"Why?"

"They're fighting over territory with the Columbians."

"So we sell it to them. Then what?"

"Then we get out of the country."

"How?"

"Assuming we're alive, I'll think of a way."

## Chapter Four

Elizabeth kept tripping over the roots and rocks on the trail. She muttered choice words every time her feet went astray, and when Hutto had enough of it, he told her to wait where she was until he came back.

Ten minutes later he appeared with a walking stick he'd made from the limb of a young oak. "Use this," he said. "And just flow with it. Don't fight it."

"Easy for you."

"This is just the start," he said. "Wear yourself out here, and we'll never make it."

He turned up the trail, leaving her to follow. He normally liked to take his time on these trails, looking at the trees, pausing at overlooks for a long gaze, listening for the chipmunks and the fiesty little squirrels everybody called boomers. But this was different.

This was life and death.

At the very least, this was life or prison. He knew he'd have a hard time with prison. The first time, those two years were enough. He'd kill himself before going back. He came close once, was actually on trial for cocaine smuggling. If he'd been on the jury, he'd have voted to convict himself. The evidence was there, even though he was innocent of that particular charge. If he'd been convicted, he might have gone to jail, or he might have taken a bottle full of little white pills. He wasn't sure, and neither was the jury, which couldn't decide on a verdict. With a hung jury, they had to let him go.

In the hall after the trial, the prosecutor met him at the water fountain. "You're mine," he said. "Someday I'll get your ass."

So far, he hadn't.

The walking stick didn't help Elizabeth much. She was fussing and cussing every step. "I don't see how I can do this with a seventy-pound load," she said.

"It'll be downhill. That makes a world of difference."

"I think we might be better off if I just stayed at the bottom and you went up *twice* after every load," she said.

"I think you'd better stop thinking."

"I can't help it. This is work."

"Think about other things. Put your mind on something else. Old boyfriends. The beauty of the mountains. What you'll do with all your money when we're out of this. Just don't think about putting one foot in front of the other."

The trail ran steadily upward. They passed through big groves of oak and spruce and birch, sprinkled with a tree local people called silverbell. If it had a real name, Hutto had never heard it.

They walked in silence. He could hear her labored breathing, and after a while, he broke into a heavy sweat. He felt his shirt sticking to his ribcage in back, under the pack. When they stopped to drink from their water bottles, he heard a woodpecker tapping at a dead tree somewhere nearby. He looked, but couldn't find it.

Elizabeth's face was tinged with red. Sweat dropped off her high cheeks. Her blonde hair hung loosely around her head, and her eyes, which he saw were a sort of green-turned-blue, were bright. He looked her over going around a switchback, and liked what he saw.

She was big and firm, with legs that were strong under her jeans. Her rear end was trim and moved with her, rather than bouncing around fighting her. Her hands were big, with short nails, and her arms were long enough to do some good if she had to protect herself.

He watched her sitting there on a big rock, blowing air past her upper lip in the direction of her nose. "You'll be okay, once you get some of that beer you've been drinking out of your system," he said.

"Hope so."

"That beer and whatever else you've been putting in there."

"I don't do any more than anybody else."

"That right?"

"That's right. You're such a smart ass."

"Just telling the truth."

"To Tell the Truth. What a joke."

He let her go first for awhile. Leading a column gives you more energy than trailing it, and knowing he was behind her made her step surer and quicker. He watched her use the walking stick with more confidence, and saw the strong legs push forward step by step.

What he knew about her amounted to nothing. Funny how you can get into a mess like this and know zip about the person with you. All he knew was she was Wilson's girl, and had been for a half year or so. When he first saw her, he thought she looked familiar, but he hadn't asked. Asking was a bit impolite. He could have seen her on a street corner, or walking the streets. He encountered strange women from time to time and usually forgot them as soon as he was done with them. Still, he wondered now if he and Elizabeth had known each other—had rumpled some sheets together—years before Wilson claimed her.

Watching her, he decided she would make it. She could hold out and carry her seventy pounds, maybe more if she had to. She led them on, ever upward, higher up this mountain named, Hutto had heard, for a man who never saw it.

With her second wind, she kept up a steady pace. Before long, they were at Rainbow Falls. She stopped at the first footbridge there and watched the water tumble eighty feet over the rocks, crashing into a small pool before continuing its way down the mountainside. Some people said that at a certain time of day, when the sun was just right, the water created a rainbow effect. Hutto had never seen it.

She stood there with one foot on the bridge, blowing air, sweating. "This place is beautiful," she said.

"You've never been here before?"

"I've never been to the mountains before," she said.

"You lived forty miles away and never went?"

"I've been to Gatlinburg, but I've never gone hiking."

"Wilson never took you?"

"Wilson never took me anyplace but to bed."

"Well, welcome to the mountains."

"Thanks."

"And on such a glorious occasion, too."

They sat for a while, watching the water fall, ever changing, always the same. A chipmunk ventured out of the rocks and teased them, always keeping at a safe distance. She wanted to feed it some crackers, but he wouldn't let her.

"These animals don't need to become dependent on human food," he said.

"If they're ever going to get dependent, they already are," she said, nodding at some candy bar wrappers on the ground.

"I don't want to add to the problem."

"You're a funny one," she said. "I can't feed the chipmunk a cracker because it's unnatural, but you're busy trying to stuff every human nose full of coke."

"Let's don't get into the morality of it."

"Why not?"

"Too deep. It has to do with choices. The human being has a choice. The chipmunk doesn't. Put a cracker out there, the chipmunk will eat it. Period. If you put some coke out there, the human has a choice."

"Put coke out there, and every human being will stuff it up his nose," she said.

"Not me."

"What do you mean, not you?"

"I mean, I don't do coke. I don't do anything."

"Why not?"

"I made my choice."

"You mean to tell me you make your living off this stuff, and you've never *used* it?"

"I've used it. I just quit, is all. I don't need it. And I don't want to get to the point where I do."

"Jesus. You're some kind of freak."

"Yes, and what a wonderful lady you are to say so."

They'd come about two and a half miles and had another four, at least, to go. Before the day was over, they'd gain 3,800 feet in elevation. They crossed the second footbridge at the falls, and went up the narrowing trail. He let her lead again. She seemed to like it, and wasn't breathing as hard anymore.

The trail began its switchbacks, climbing the slope along the contour. From some of the points you could see for miles on a good day. This wasn't a good day. What you saw was mostly gray. He thought it might rain.

They passed through rhododendron, a massive wall

of it, and came into the spruce-fir forest. Up this high, the plants were similar to those growing in Canada. That's what the colder weather and higher elevation did. At some point, the oaks and birch stopped, and the big spruce and firs took over. The vegetation here was more sparse, reflecting its struggle with the elements.

She stopped walking at a rocky point and sat down, watching a hawk flitting above the treetops. "How much further?" she asked.

"A mile at most."

"Do you even know where that package is?"

"Sure. Up there."

"You haven't even used that gizmo of yours. The stuff could be way the hell over yonder."

"It's not," he said, and took off his pack. He removed the Klecko, turned it on, and watched the red light beat faster, with the clicking more frantic when the device pointed straight up the mountain.

"I was kind of hoping we might stumble across it somewhere down here," she said.

"No, I tried to drop on the ridge tops to make it easier to find."

"Thanks a lot."

"At your service."

They went on, and the trail grew steeper, the rocks underfoot sharper. Concentrating on keeping their footing, they said nothing. He could hear her breathing again, this time deeper than before, struggling for oxygen in the thinner air. Before reaching the top, he stopped her and took another reading on the Klecko. It pointed them upward. He took the lead this time, and stopped every couple hundred yards to get his bearings.

They reached the top, pausing briefly to congratulate themselves, and walked on to Le Conte Lodge, a group of log cabins around a couple of bigger log structures. Hutto had stayed here several times, paying sixty dollars for the privilege of lying on a rope bed listening to mice scrambling around your shack. Once, in April, it was so cold he spent most of the night fussing with the little stove to keep the girl he was with from freezing, and never got to sleep at all. The girl, a big strong blonde not unlike Elizabeth, had packed up two bottles of cheap champagne, which she drank after the meat stew supper, and then drifted off to sleep about 2:00 A.M., after complaining about the cold for several hours. He'd perched on the straight-back wooden chair by her bunk, fussed with the heater, and looked for mice, which he could hear but couldn't see. He couldn't stand mice. Give him a bear anytime rather than a mouse.

They stopped off by the lodge to fill their water bottles, then moved quickly up the trail. The views from the lodge were fabulous, but this day was cloudy. In all the times he'd been there, he'd never had a good day for the view. Some people claimed to have seen Knoxville from there, but it was usually so cloudy and foggy that he was lucky to see his boots.

No road ran to the lodge. Supplies came in on

horseback, sometimes by helicopter. The people working there were curious about everyone stopping by, so he and Elizabeth didn't pause long. After they got away from the lodge unchallenged, he checked the Klecko again. It told him what they wanted was located a little to the north side of the trail, somewhat downhill. So he led her off through the overgrowth. She worried about getting lost, and he just held up his right hand to silence her. Now he had the tracking device out in his left hand and they were drawing close to the package.

He slowed down, making less noise in the brush, creeping forward. If some park rangers were there waiting for him by the coke, he wanted to spot them first. They still had time to turn around, take what they stuffed in the hollow tree at the foot of the mountain, and make a run for it.

Then he heard the noise. Lots of it. It sounded like grunts and squeals, a pigpen run amuck. He couldn't figure it. They crouched in the small trees awhile, listening. Then he crawled to the other side, motioning Elizabeth on with him. When he saw what was happening, he sat back, too surprised to talk.

What he saw was a bear.

A big black bear. The kind he'd rather face than a mouse. This bear had found their package of coke, ripped it apart, and eaten every bit of its contents. Now he was rolling along the ground, trying to roar but only getting out a sound like a hog might make.

"Ate the coke," Hutto said. "Ate it all."

"Boy, he's really high."

"He's dying."

"It's killing him?"

"Wouldn't 140 pounds kill *you?*"

"Can't you do something?"

"What we can do is wait and watch until he's a goner, then see if he left us anything."

"I can't believe he ate that much."

"Well, you know what they say. Once you get started, you just can't stop," Hutto said.

They sat there, watching the bear pass through agony into a kind of fitful daydream, while his muscles twitched and his nose snorted and little whimpering noises came from his mouth. Then, when Hutto decided it was all over, they went to take a look.

He hadn't left them a gram.

Every package was opened. A lot had spilled onto the ground, fertilizing the clumps of tundra grass trying to grow there. Elizabeth wanted to scoop some up and save it, but he wouldn't let her. Instead, he gave her a survival knife and they both worked on digging a hole to bury the parachute and what was left of the pack and the brown bags it had carried.

That done, they started back up the hill to the trail. "Boy, some big planner you are," she said.

"Well, you don't think about cocaine-freak bears."

"What do you think of?"

"What I think of is getting out of this thing alive."

"Okay. That's one down, four to go," she said.

"Why don't you just be quiet?"

"Poor bear," she said.

"Damn dumb bear," he muttered, and they found the trail again, running along the ridge top. Go to the left and you wind up in Georgia. Go right and you'll eventually come to Maine. He wanted to avoid the lodge, so they went right, briefly. He'd double back to the Jeep on the Bullhead.

## Chapter Five

Fewer people take Bullhead. It's a little longer hike, and most think every step counts, particularly uphill. The trail is named for the ridge of Mount Le Conte it runs along. Somebody thought it looked like a bull's head; Hutto had never seen it that way. He'd looked at it on the scale model of the mountains at Sugarlands, the park's visitor center, and he could never see the bull in its outline.

Now they'd be going down it. It would be seven miles. He could make it in two hours or less, by himself. But it looked like rain. They couldn't see any of the celebrated view from the mountaintop, and fog was settling in hard on the summit. Hutto figured it would rain, just to make life more interesting.

They'd gone a half mile when the downpour began. Hutto had been in the lead, nearly jogging downhill. Elizabeth managed to keep up. They passed some magnificent red spruce and towering Fraser firs, but he was hurrying too much to consider them.

She kept pace, surprising him, until the rain started. When the trail got muddy, she began slipping.

She'd give little squeals when she got near a steep edge, and finally sat down in the center of the trail, ignoring the mud.

"I can't make it in this," she said.

He looked at her. Her blonde hair hung wet and loose. Her shirt was plastered to her chest. Her jeans were a mess.

"We have to move," he said.

"Can't."

The rain roared down in sheets. He could barely see past where they were. The drops were cold, just released from their clouds.

"You're going to have to do it," he said. "When they find that bear, they're going to be looking for us."

"I'm afraid."

"It's all right. It's nothing to be afraid of."

"But I feel like I'm going to slip over the edge," she said.

"We'll go slower. Just take each step as carefully as you can. Get traction on the rocks. Take your time. But we have to keep going."

"Is this supposed to be fun?"

"Nobody said anything about fun."

"But people do it for fun?"

"That's right. They feel like they're being challenged by something bigger than they are, but all the time they're really safe. Probably safer than they are at home."

"Then what are we doing?"

"For us, it's not safe. For us, there really are bears in the woods."

She got up. He walked close to her, and she held onto his hand to keep her balance. Further down, though it still rained, she wasn't so scared, and the trail grew wider, less frightening. The drop to the side was nothing, and sometimes they walked on flat ground. She began to giggle and slide intentionally, pulling him with her.

They fell in the goop several times, and she whooped, "Mountain mud-wrestling."

He wanted to tell her to cut it out, to shut up, and hurry. But he didn't. It had been a long time since anybody had teased him that way, almost like a child. And he couldn't remember ever wrestling in the mud with a strong-limbed female person while the rain poured down, the sweet heady smell of spruce and fir and the great outdoors covered everything.

She felt interesting, soft but firm. He wouldn't mind rolling around in the mud a little while with that soft firmness. Sure, she was the late lamented Wilson's girl, but by now Wilson was laid out in the county morgue in Sevierville, with a covey of cops standing around trying to figure out his devious purpose. It could have been Hutto, had he lacked the good sense to avoid overloading himself for his jump. Though Wilson wasn't exactly his buddy, and definitely wasn't almost a brother, as Elizabeth had described him, they had shared a lot. But not this girl, not Elizabeth. They'd never passed her around like some men did their women. Hutto had never gone in for that.

Though she looked good enough in her way, Hutto

had never paid her much attention. She was Wilson's girl, and beyond his interest. He might have looked at her a few times. He might have admired those legs as she lounged around in jogging shorts, and he might have been intrigued by what shook beneath her bikini top at the pool, but he'd never seriously thought about her.

Now she was all he could think about, the way her flesh felt underneath her cotton shirt, and the crazy laugh she let go while sliding in the mud, intent on taking him down with her. He decided to let her. If she wanted him in the mud with her, he'd oblige. Here he was, working toward $150 million, minus what the bear took, and all he could think about was this woman and what she might offer if he remained on good behavior. He liked her fullness, the bigness of her, and the way she moved. He liked her skin and the way it felt when she stripped the shirt off, and he liked the way she flopped and squirmed beneath him.

Right now she was the muddiest woman he'd ever seen and certainly the loveliest. She laughed, she giggled, she tickled and squealed.

She grabbed him and led him inside her, right there in the mud while the rain streamed down, and he thought maybe this was how God felt creating the earth, with the thundering elements all around, part of your love.

He'd heard how danger made sex better, how sometimes people craved sex just before death, wanted to take one last shot at eternity before lights out, and he wondered if this was somehow like that. He couldn't have lasted long, but however long it was, it was long enough, because she was soon holding both his shoulders and bumping his chin with her forehead, gasping for breath.

"Oh, Lord," she said. "Oh, God. That was a first. That was it. The real thing."

He settled down beside her, naked, face up toward the downpour. She rested her head on his chest, wet hair falling everywhere.

"What a damn fine woman," he said. "I want to know everything about you, what your dreams are, all that stuff."

"Maybe there'll be time for that, if we make it."

"Visualize something strong enough, and it comes true."

"Sometimes it doesn't."

"But sometimes it does," he said. "I believe in the power of positive dreams."

"I believe in the power of positive drinking."

"That sounds like a country song."

The rain stopped and the footing got better. By the time they reached the Bullhead ridge itself, the ground was nearly dry. They stopped at a little heath bald, drinking from their water bottles. Here, for once, there was a view. The rainclouds lifted, the sunlight flew golden and warm, a few patches of blue showed overhead, and they could look across the range to Sugarland Mountain toward the southwest, and further on, Blanket Mountain.

The bald was thick with rhododendron, mountain laurel, and a few azaleas. The ridge tops through the

Smokies were full of balds, several acres of reasonably clear land where no large trees grew. Some were mostly grass; others, like this one, had shrubs. The Cherokee Indians had an old tradition that something like a bird of fire had burned them. The white man's biologists and botanists couldn't figure them out. Maybe they were caused by lightning fires. Early settlers grazed cattle on them, keeping vegetation down.

Some of the old-timers called them hells. Hutto guessed that was because the ones with shrubs were so tangled, you could get in a hell of a mess trying to get through one.

Elizabeth looked at the view awhile, then inspected the plants. She got on her knees to look at some little purple flowers.

"Sometime I'd like to do this just for fun," she said. "Something about it makes me feel good."

"If you do any hiking after this, it'll have to be in the Alps or the Andes or somewhere like that."

Then she found a nest of snakes. He looked them over, huddled together in thick grass beneath a rhododendron, and decided they were baby king snakes, though he wasn't sure. He'd never been a snake expert. He did know that only two types of poisonous snakes lived in these mountains, the timber rattlesnake and copperheads. He was positive these weren't rattlesnakes, but not so sure they weren't copperheads. So he backed off.

"Aren't you going to kill them?" she asked.

"They didn't bother us. We found them, not vice versa."

"But they're snakes."

"Yeah, but you don't kill things unless you have to. You kill for meat, or you kill to stay alive. I wasn't going to eat them, and they weren't going to hurt us. So what's the point?"

Beneath the clouds the sun dropped steadily, and Hutto turned down the trail again with Elizabeth close behind. She had no trouble keeping up now, matching his quick steps. When he looked around at her, she was busy watching things off the trail, paying no attention to the rocks and roots. Her feet set themselves down easily now, naturally finding the right spot.

She'd be sore later on. The lactic acid would build in her leg muscles and lower back so that she'd have trouble moving at all after sleeping. But that was yet to come. He'd let her roll now while she could.

The slope of the mountain came rising toward them below the cloud line, the tops of the trees green and fluttering in the wind, thick enough to hide everything under their canopy. At the bottom was Cherokee Orchard, the Jeep, and the hollow tree with their seventy pounds of coke. Of the five trails going to the top of Mount Le Conte, only Bullhead and Rainbow Falls shared a common starting point. With the dead bear and scattered coke up on top, Hutto was glad they didn't have to retrace their steps down the mountain. If rangers or somebody from the lodge found the bear, they could radio for enforcement rangers or the sheriff to search for suspects.

Now he worried about what they'd find at the Jeep.

It was registered in Elizabeth's name, but even the dullest cop could figure out that she was Wilson's girlfriend and come looking for them. If they had a welcoming party at the Jeep, Hutto figured he'd turn around, walk through the backcountry, and in a couple of days come out somewhere near Pigeon Forge. They could steal a car and drive to Chattanooga or Bristol or Asheville, and take a bus or plane to some resort where they could blend in with the crowd.

He didn't want to kill anybody. He kept telling himself that, feeling the weight of the pistols in his pack. Not even $150 million was enough for him to kill. For some people, $150 is enough. For him, money was nothing much, just paper and ink, something that let you fool the world.

He wondered which type Elizabeth was, the killing type or the sensible type. It might not bother her. Sometimes those eyes, with their indeterminate color, had a hard look. That disturbed him. Maybe he'd have to soften them up.

When they reached bottom, they kept walking to the Jeep. "What about the tree? What about the tree?" he heard her whispering as they plodded along.

"Wait until it's clear," he said.

Nothing was unusual at the parking area. A young couple was packing stuff away in a Toyota with Alabama license plates, and an older couple was standing near a big Oldsmobile watching two young grandsons squabble about bears.

"Howdy," the old man said.

"How's it going?" Hutto said.

"Rainy day for a hike."

"Pretty muddy," Hutto said.

"How far'd you go?" one of the grandsons asked.

"To the top."

"Wow. We only went up to that little log bridge."

"You'll do better next time."

"Grandma won't go," the kid said. "No bathrooms up there."

Elizabeth sat in the driver's seat. She took off her boots and collapsed, putting her head on the steering wheel. "What about the tree?" she said.

"I'll go," he said. "Anything happens, anybody shows up, any trouble at all, you leave. Hear?"

She nodded. He walked back up the trail, crossed the footbridge, and sat under a tulip poplar for fifteen minutes, watching. Nothing stirred. Then he loaded his pack, hoisted it onto his back, staggering under the new weight, and went back to the parking lot.

Everyone was gone except Elizabeth. He saw her head on the steering wheel, asleep. Only, what if she's not asleep? he thought. What if she's dead? What if some Colombian hit man or wild cop had already found her?

But they hadn't. She woke up as he slid into the passenger seat. "Ready to roll?" he asked.

"God, I could sleep for a month."

"Just tonight. Tomorrow we do it all over again, only it'll be harder."

"Hell."

She started the engine. Hutto half expected it to blow up from a dynamite bomb planted on the starter. But it didn't. He decided he'd been reading too many spy novels. Too much John Le Carre, too much Trevanian.

It was downhill most of the way back to Gatlinburg. She coasted, steering hard on the curves. The road was one lane, one way. Normally her driving would have given him a scare. Now, with the sun going down and the mountain blacking out behind them, he didn't care. He just wanted to find a bed and a bath.

They pulled in at one of the smaller motels. He got a single room, one bed, two persons, and paid cash for it. The clerk asked for no identification, so he signed his name, "John Foster, Montgomery, Ala."

The room was small, the bed caved in at the middle. She didn't complain. She took a shower first, came out wearing a towel, and crawled beneath the covers. When he got cleaned up, he put on the spare pair of jeans with the clean shirt he'd been carrying in the pack and walked across the street to a little store and bought a newspaper. The late edition of the Knoxville *News-Sentinel* had a story about Wilson. "The mysterious chutist," the story called him. From the sound of it, the reporter, at least, hadn't figured out what was going on. They had Wilson pegged, but nobody could decide just what he was up to. They seemed to think he was just getting away, somehow, with seventy pounds of cocaine.

He carried the paper to the Burger King down the

street, ate two cheeseburgers, and read the rest. Most of the story was devoted to Wilson's Vietnam War background, telling about the medals he'd won. Since the war he'd been unsettled, the story said. Much of his activity was unaccounted for. Even his family didn't know what he was doing. Clearly a case of another life ruined by the terrible war experience.

Let 'em think that if they want, Hutto thought.

He flipped the page and saw a story in the bottom right-hand corner titled, "Strange Crash in Carolina." He read it and knew right away that there was a terrible mistake. The Cessna hadn't made it to the ocean. It hadn't made it far at all. Something went wrong. It only got to Black Mountain, North Carolina—barely out of the Smokies—where it crashed on the mountain, just missing some vacation cabins. The people there had come running out to make a brave effort at saving the pilot and passengers, only to find there was no pilot and no passengers. Lo and behold, the plane was empty.

The fire put itself out, and the authorities found no identification in the plane, no trace of anything. They'd never seen anything like it.

But Hutto was sure that by this time tomorrow, the DEA, FBI, and even the Pigeon Forge cops—who had never seen anything like the mysterious chutist—would have connected Wilson with the Black Mountain Cessna now mystifying the cops on the other side of the hills. Of course, the plane couldn't be traced to Hutto, but that wouldn't matter.

The Colombians who were going to take delivery

over on the Cumberland Plateau would know for sure something funny was going on. They'd know Wilson jumped, and they'd know Hutto jumped, and that they scammed the coke. They'd know Hutto was out there somewhere running around putting together a huge coke deal.

One thing nobody did was skin the Colombians. They knew how to turn you inside out and keep you alive the whole time. They'd make you happy to get the opportunity to put a bullet in your ear.

That's why he and Wilson had planned to just disappear, leaving no trace of the plane. If the Colombians had a clue, they'd find you. If they could smell you, they'd tree you. Now things were changed even more, and the plan had already altered so much it made him uncomfortable.

Cops didn't worry him so much. He figured he could outsmart cops. But Colombians worried him. They were tough, they were mean, they didn't give up, and they hated to have their pride kicked in the teeth.

He wasn't sure what to do, so he just picked up some burgers for Elizabeth. But she was already asleep, so he sat there eating her fries, drinking a 7-Up, wondering what would happen now. When he lay down beside her, lifting the sheet and bedspread carefully, she didn't stir. He hardly noticed her lying there, still in the towel and mostly covered up. But in his dreams he saw a big blonde woman dancing and rolling in a huge mud puddle. She laughed with him, and when he joined her, she put a hand grenade in his mouth and rolled away, cackling and howling, as it blew up. He woke, chilled, and turned down the air conditioner.

When he stretched out on the bed again, she tossed a few times, mumbled something, and rested an arm on his chest. Damn it all, he thought, damn if he'd be run off by a dream. This is real. Next thing he knew, it was morning.

## Chapter Six

She was awake when he got out of the shower.

"Can't move," she said.

A sheet covered her. Tangled hair spread across her pillow. "God, I hurt so bad," she said.

"Thought you'd be sore."

"Sore ain't the word for it."

"When you move around, the soreness will go away."

"No way am I getting out of this bed."

"Come on, we have work to do."

"Why traipse through those hills just to watch a bear eat the stuff?"

"That was a quirk of fate. Just one of those things."

"That bear must have felt real good."

"Yeah. So good he died."

"What a way to go, though."

"Dead's dead," Hutto said.

She struggled to get up. "Lie there first and stretch the muscles. Bend your feet around to work the calves loose. Then take a hot bath. I'm going to get breakfast," he said.

When he got back with a bag of sausage biscuits, she was getting out the tub. "It worked, sort of," she said.

"Always does."

"How do you know so much?"

"I've been in and out of shape so many times, I've spent half my life sore."

"I don't believe it. When were you out of shape?"

"Last time? About two years ago. Had to lose sixty pounds. I go through these periods where I lose control and eat and drink and lie around the house all day until I look like a slob. At that point it's either give up and be a roll of blubber the rest of my life, or start running and lifting weights again. So far, I can always get back into it."

"You can't get that fat if you do all this hiking."

"I don't hike then. I just ride up into the mountains and look at things, then ride back to town."

"I guess that's my problem. I'm too out of shape."

"No, your shape isn't bad at all. You're just not used to this much exercise. By the time this week is over, you'll be feeling good."

"A lot of good it'll do me, sitting in jail."

"Think positive."

"Good vibes."

"Right."

"Good aura."

"Something like that."

"Bonnie and Clyde probably thought positive, too.

Look what happened to them."

"Well, they had a lot of problems."

"So?"

"So, we don't have those problems."

"I don't know where you get all this mystical crap."

"There's nothing mystical about positive thoughts. More people should have them."

Hutto hated to hear himself talk like that. He didn't like sounding like some Indian guru, particularly not around Elizabeth. Sure, people *should* think positively, but they ought to quit bad jobs, dump bad marriages, kick bad kids in the seat of the pants, move out of bad towns, and stop dropping dollar bills in the collection plates of bad churches. But it'll never happen.

She finished her biscuits, washed down with Dr Pepper from the drink machine in the hallway, and he demonstrated how to stretch her muscles to loosen them enough to hike. He had her bending and twisting, and finished her up with the hurdler's exercise, sitting on the floor with one leg extended before her and the other twisted behind. He'd been a hurdler once, years ago, though he preferred running with both feet firmly on the track.

He drove past the Jeep today, pulling out of Gatlinburg, heading the park visitors' center, driving through the loop where the road doubled back over itself climbing a hill, and stopped in the Alum Cave trail parking lot.

"Where's this trail go?" she asked.

"Same place we went yesterday."

"Why didn't we stay up there, then? There was that lodge up there."

He stared at her a minute and blew a stream of air between the gap in his upper front teeth.

"I don't think I can climb up there two days in a row," she said.

"This package isn't all the way to the top, if my calculations are right. When you drop a package from a plane in the dark, it's hard to tell just where it's going. But this hike shouldn't be as hard."

"Thank sweet Jesus for that."

They walked up the trail about a quarter mile, crossing two footbridges, and he went into a thick stand of rhododendron and hid the cocaine, taking it quickly from his pack, burying it in a pile of last year's leaves.

"What if it rains on it?" she asked.

"It won't."

"How do you know?"

"That rhododendron will act just like an umbrella."

"What if a bear gets it?"

"Don't 'what if' me to death. Just get moving."

The first part of the trail was easy. There was the usual rhododendron and mountain laurel. The trail crisscrossed a little creek called Styx Creek several times. They stepped on rocks to keep their boots dry. Alum Cave Creek, the main body of water here, was a curious thing with nothing living in it, not even moss. Iron ore in the water keeps it clean, or dead, depending on how you look at it.

Back in 1951, the year after Hutto was born, a big rain tore up this area. Alum Cave Creek became a wild thing, ripping huge trees up by the roots, tossing boulders about, changing its banks forever. The remains of some of those old trees still rotted on the forest floor.

After going a mile and a half, they passed through Arch Rock. The rock was slate and the middle had washed out. Following the trail up through its slippery center, they held onto a wire put up by the Park Service, and moved on, more uphill now.

A half mile further, they found another little bald and an overlook. "Look at that," he said, and pointed out Keyhole Rock. It was an opening, a window, on a narrow humpbacked ridge extending down the mountain.

"What caused that?" she asked.

"Water, maybe, and wind. Who knows?"

"These mountains are weird," she said.

"Not weird, just old. Once they were twice as tall as the Rockies. Erosion and time have worn them down. They're so old that rivers once ran where these mountaintops are."

"How do you know that?"

"I just know."

He took the Klecko out of his pack, turned it on, and took a reading. "I think it's over there. Somewhere around the Keyhole," he said.

"How are you going to get it from there?"

"Just try, girl, just try."

"So it's girl again."

"Sorry. Bad habit."

"I don't call you boy."

"I know. I said I was sorry."

They went uphill another quarter mile and came to Alum Cave. It wasn't a cave at all, but like so many things here, had been misnamed. More bluff than anything, it was coated with alum and other minerals. He sat beneath the overhang and pulled sandwiches from his pack.

"Roast beef?" he asked.

"Where did you get these things?"

"I do my shopping early."

It had taken nearly three hours to get here. By himself, he could have done it in under two. He wanted to pack out at least two sets of the coke today.

"Okay, eat up so we can roll on," he said.

They watched a hawk flit back and forth, its wild cry harsh against the breeze, soaring toward Keyhole Rock and back overhead.

"To think all this was up here all the time and I never went hiking," she said. "It'd be nice just to come here and enjoy it some time."

"Enjoy it now."

"Sure."

"Put your mind on other things."

"Like that hawk," she said. "It'd be great to be a bird. If you didn't like someplace, you could just fly away."

"You can do that now."

"No, you can't."

"Everybody can, but they won't. They think they have responsibilities."

"It seems like flying would make it easier to go."

"There were peregrine falcons here once," he said.

"What happened to them?"

"Long gone. Maybe they got sick of it and flew away."

"Maybe they died out," she said.

"Could be. They're rare everywhere now. The Park Service is trying to re-establish them but I bet it won't work. If they didn't want to live here fifty years ago, they won't now, either."

Other hikers came through. Some wanted to talk it up, pleased to be outdoors and surviving the hike. Others, dead tired, plodded right past the bluff with scarcely a look at it. Most asked one question, "How far to the top?"

"About three miles," Hutto told them. "All uphill."

"Lots of people on this trail," Elizabeth said.

"It's short and easy to get to."

"They must have read about Wilson."

"Who can put two and two together? We might as well suspect them as them suspect us. We look like a happy couple out for a walk in the woods."

They finished their sandwiches, drank some water, and walked to the part of the trail where the path to Keyhole Rock began.

"Wait a minute. I'm not going out there," she said.

"It's easy, just like walking across your kitchen floor."

"That's more like running on a knife edge."

"Don't be nervous. It's not that dangerous."

"You've done this before?"

"Many times, sweetie. Many times."

"You're a nut."

"Just follow me. Step where I do."

The steep ridge rose to a point at their feet. Below, they saw boulders that had lost their grasp eons ago and tumbled until catching on bigger rocks. Little trees clung to the sides, crabbing a half-life from the poor soil.

He heard her breath pump in and out sharply, and he wondered if he should have let her go first so that he could grab her if she fell. But it was too late to turn around.

"People can see us," she said.

"So what? We're just nature lovers out for a better look."

"It's like walking a tightrope."

"Just keep smiling."

He brought the Klecko out when they were halfway along the spine. It indicated the package was a bit further, apparently off the end of the cliff beyond the keyhole itself.

"Isn't this fun?" he said.

"Fool. Dummy. Stupid idiot."

"Aren't you having a good time?"

"If I survive this, I'm going to whip up on you."

"Sounds like fun."

"Weirdo."

They slowly made their way to the keyhole, and looked down through it at both sides of the world. The wind zipped through it. "I've never seen anything like this," she said.

"Stick with me, and you'll see the wonders of the world."

"Sticking with you is becoming a problem."

"Such wit and charm."

"What does that gizmo of yours say?"

"It says our prize is somewhere straight down there."

"Way down there?"

"Who knows?"

"I'm not going down there. Not even for $150 million, minus what the bear ate."

"Good, because I want you to stay here."

He took a thin mountaineering rope from his pack, made a sling in one end to fit around his chest, then secured it to a steady, firm rock near the keyhole. He put on a pair of goatskin rappel gloves that had cost too much, and got set to go.

"How'd you learn to do this?" she asked.

"Thank Uncle Sam. He taught me just about all I know."

"What if the rope isn't long enough?"

"What if, what if."

He shoved off the edge, away from the side of the keyhole that hikers could see. He dropped, and dropped, and dropped, and the rope wasn't long enough.

Looking up, he could see her watching. He gave her a little wave and smile, then braced against the side of the wall, and saw the chute caught in a bush not far away. He eased along a small ledge to the flat place where the package rested. On his knees, he opened it up, relieved to see some woods creature hadn't beaten him to it. Then he took off his pack and loaded it. Since the climb back to the top would be tough, he decided to split the load into quarters, hauling thirty-five pounds at a time back to the keyhole.

He climbed four times, up and down, loading and unloading his big pack in silence. Elizabeth sat Indian-style and looked on. When he came up for the last time, she still hadn't touched any of the brown paper packages.

"Well, load up," he said.

"How many million is that worth?"

"A lot."

"I want to know. How many?"

"Oh, sixty, I guess, if you know the right people."

"God. What a crazy world this is."

"You're right there."

"This is enough to feed Africa for a week."

"At least."

"This is nuts. The world's gone crazy."

"Seems I've heard that before," he said.

"Lunatics, lunatics, lunatics," she said in a quiet

little singsong.

He let her go on and on. She's right, he knew. She's right.

## Chapter Seven

The full load was too much for her. So, though it required tight packing, he took eighty pounds and gave her sixty. That was still nearly too heavy. She staggered a little, but it couldn't be helped. Wilson, big as he was, would have had a tough time carrying all that weight. Elizabeth weighed 125 pounds less than he did. Hutto wondered how she did it.

She tripped once on the thin spine of the ridge and looked like she would fall over the edge, flipping down in a crazy top-heavy spin. But she caught herself with one hand, pushed forward, and kept walking.

Hutto's load, along with his guns and gear, was almost more than he could handle. It felt like he was carrying the Prussian army back there. He'd paid nearly three hundred dollars for this backpack. It was the biggest one he could find, and right now seemed like a bargain. It was a Lowe Special Expedition Pack, designed for long-distance duty. He had removed the horizontal divider inside it, making it into one big bag except for the small pockets where he kept the pistols, rope, water bottle, and some other goodies.

This was indeed lunatic business, he decided, looking down each side at the treetops far below. People do crazy things just for the hell of it, to see if they can make it. They can't explain just why they climb Mount Everest, or why they sit in a sardine can circling the earth, or why they fly off Niagara Falls inside a barrel.

"Why'd you do it, mister?" the TV guy would ask.

The hero would shrug and spit and shuffle and say, "Uh, gee, well, see, you had to be there to know."

What the hell could the answer be? Why else was he here? He already had enough money. Not more money than he could ever spend. No, he could run through a million in a week if he had to. But he didn't have to, and he had enough hidden away that he'd make it to old age just fine if he never worked another day or stole another thing.

He did it, he guessed, to show the real bad guys they could be whipped. The money would be nice, a perfect touch. The money was the real issue. Funny how five or six hundred pounds of distilled coca leaf juice can turn the world inside out. It was a game, a game for keeps.

"How'd you pull it off?" the TV guy would ask.

"Just outsmarted 'em," he'd say. Except that only he would know. He'd never be able to tell anyone, or he was a dead man, and somehow that seemed the greatest pleasure of all, one to keep entirely to himself.

Or to Elizabeth and himself. He worried about having her here. Wilson could handle himself. Wilson might not have been the smartest guy around, but he'd know enough not to talk and get himself in trouble. Elizabeth might talk, or she might not.

When he and Wilson planned this, they decided a third person was crucial, though they tried to work it out every other way. Wilson wanted to dump her when it was over. All he could talk about were the Scandinavian sweeties and the Tahitian beauties. Elizabeth wasn't enough for Wilson.

He had to talk Wilson into giving her a million bucks to keep her quiet. Wilson just wanted to leave her behind to take the heat. He might even have killed her. Hutto wasn't sure. On occasion Wilson could be mean, senselessly cruel. Hutto figured Elizabeth deserved a chance to get away, too, even while Wilson was still around.

Hutto always wondered what women like Elizabeth saw in guys like Wilson. Must have been the drugs and the money. Coke, mucho bucks, a nice house, and a big garage full of Corvettes and Porsches impressed a lot of airhead women. Elizabeth didn't seem to fit the job description, but you can't figure them, Hutto thought. You never know what they're going to do. Some of them have a hunger for the wild life that can't be filled. They go on from party to party, bar to bar, man to man, until one day a longhaul trucker from Ohio finds a body in a culvert on Interstate 75.

Up ahead, she stopped in the middle of the path. She started to turn toward him. "Don't turn around," he said. "You'll get disoriented."

"Next time," he heard her say. "Next time one of you bastards starts talking about needing a little help on something, no big deal, just drive the Jeep, I'm going to run the other direction."

"Won't be any next time."

"I hear you."

"There won't."

"There'll always be a next time. I can see you now, old and gray over in Switzerland, trying to figure how to rob the Swiss bank. You'll sit down and wonder who can help you, and you'll call up old Elizabeth. She always was a sucker for idiot stunts."

"Just keep walking."

"How do I get involved in these things?"

"Just one foot in front of the other. Go on," he said. "We've got to get down so we can start all over again."

They made it to the point where Keyhole Ridge joined the main trail and turned right, hardly paused at Alum Cave, waved to some other hikers, and headed down the trail. Every step was so heavy, Hutto felt like he would plunge right into the earth and wind up swimming in the molten core. But they still made it down in an hour and a half. Neither said a word the whole way.

Back at the Jeep he unloaded the stuff into two of the suitcases Elizabeth brought along for this duty, then set off back up the trail to the rhododendron thicket where he'd stored the original seventy pounds. She caught up with him, lighter on her feet with an empty pack. While he split the coke between them, hiding in the brush, she watched. A drop of sweat hung on her upper lip.

She curled her tongue up and licked it off. It reminded him of a lizard. A lovely one.

"Why don't we just take what we have and leave the rest?" she said.

"And kill off half the bear population?"

"I'm serious."

"So am I."

"We can go now and still get away. If we can't live on $60 million or $100 million or whatever it is, we don't deserve it."

"No,"

"If we get out now, we can still make it. Nobody has figured out we're in it yet, I bet."

"I think we better carry it through to the end."

"What if I want out?" she said. "What if you just cut me out with my share, and you go on and do whatever you want?"

"We're in this together."

"But I don't want to be in it together."

"Look," he said. "I'm sorry you had to get involved. But you're here, and there's nothing that can be done about it."

"It's a free country, isn't it? I can just walk down this trail and get in my Jeep and go."

"No, you can't."

"What do you mean, no, I can't?"

"I mean I can't let you do that."

"You'd stop me."

"Yes."

"How."

"However I had to."

"You'd kill me?"

"I don't know."

"I thought you said you'd never killed anybody. Except in Vietnam."

"I meant to say I'd never killed anybody who didn't deserve it."

"You son of a bitch."

"Sorry."

"You've kidnapped me."

"If that's what you want to call it."

"That's against the law."

"Laws don't seem to bother us much."

"Who are you—Jesse James?"

He stared her down. "You'll be set for life if we can just get through this," he said.

"I'd be set for life with what's in the pack right here. Several lifetimes."

"Probably."

"So what's the point?"

"The point is that we're going to do what we set out to do. The point is that they could kill us just as dead over what's in this pack as over the whole thing. We might as well go for it."

"I don't understand."

"You will when it's over."

"This is a war for you, isn't it? This is a little Vietnam right here in the Smokies."

"Wrongo. I'm not one of these crazy-ass Vietnam vets who can't get over the war. They sit around drinking beer all day until they flip out and blow away the kids and the old lady."

"Something's eating you."

"I don't want to hear that talk. Period."

"You're sick."

"I'm fine. It's the world that's gone crazy. Who said that? You? Me? Waylon Jennings? The old things don't count anymore. The new things don't matter. Who do you trust? Nobody. How many sheriffs have we had just right here in east Tennessee who are in prison for selling coke? Six, seven, something like that? Cops can't investigate murders because they're too busy selling dope. Somebody robs your house, nobody cares. Cop'll come out, sit there in the chair, drink your coffee, and say it's too bad, but you might as well kiss it all good-bye because they'll never find the thief."

"What's this have to do with us?"

"Everything. It's just part of the same big picture. There aren't any good guys any more. There are a lot of gray guys, with black and white all mixed up. We're all in it. The businessman taking from his company, the salesman cheating on his expenses, the farmer living on government handouts. No good guys. No bad guys. Just guys trying to get by."

"You're wrong there," she said. "There are bad guys. Some real bad guys."

"I know. Guys so bad you can't even imagine it. Maybe it's more like there aren't any good guys. Just some guys are badder than others."

"A lot badder."

"Right."

"You're not that bad, are you?"

"No. I'm trying to stay away from them."

"You're really going to go through with this?"

"You bet."

"Maybe you better show me how to shoot one of those guns."

"Later. Let's get back to the Jeep. Being gone so long makes me nervous."

"What happened to Mister Cool's nerves?"

"They're ringing like a telephone cable."

They crossed the two footbridges and returned to

the parking lot on the main road. Hutto led the way through the trees toward the Jeep, then stopped when he saw a man working at the door lock on the passenger side. Slipping off the backpack, Hutto removed a pistol from one of its pockets, and eased forward, first from tree to tree, then from car to car. No one else was in the parking lot.

When he came out from behind a Buick with Michigan plates next to the Jeep, the guy still fumbling with the lock had decided to say to hell with it and just break the glass. He turned to get a rock and saw Hutto creeping toward him. He began to run, heading down a little embankment toward the creek. Hutto was right behind him, pistol in hand.

The guy was young and quick with long dirty blonde hair, a baseball cap worn backwards, jeans, a Confederate flag T-shirt, and wearing old four-stripe K-mart-style running shoes. Hutto would never have caught him, if he hadn't tripped on a rock by the creek and fallen into the water.

Then Hutto was on him, popping the pistol barrel across his forehead. The thief squirmed, kicking, writhing, until Hutto slammed a chop into his neck. That brought him to a halt. Hutto eased up a little. He didn't want to knock him out, though he wouldn't have minded killing him.

"Who you with?" Hutto demanded.

"What?"

Hutto slapped the pistol barrel across his face. The sight caught the upper lip and tore away some of the boy's skin, leaving bright blood pouring onto his teeth.

"Who you working for?" Hutto said.

"Screw you," the kid muttered.

"I'll kill you right here. Right now. Unless you tell me."

"Don't work for nobody," he said.

"Like hell."

He slapped his face. The kid came to life a little, so Hutto chopped him again. His brown eyes bulged and the skin around them turned bright red. Hutto thought he might have popped a blood vessel, but he didn't really care.

"Name 'em."

"Who?"

"Your bosses."

"Ain't got no bosses," the kid said. "Let me go, son of a bitch."

Hutto slammed his head into a rock.

"Jesus, you're killing me."

"Not yet," Hutto said.

"Crazy bastard. You crazy, that's what."

"What were you doing with that Jeep."

"Tape deck. Wanted your tape deck."

"Tape deck?"

"Yeah, man, twenty-five bucks for a good tape deck."

Hutto slapped his face again, this time from both sides, left to right, and right to left. He put his hand around the kid's throat and closed it tight on the windpipe. The kid squealed, making a high-pitched little scream that went nowhere. Then he was quiet.

Hutto let go and watched him gulp air as the life seeped back into him. He sat back on his heels so he didn't have to touch the kid.

When the kid looked like he'd live, Hutto asked,

"What's your name?"

"Axel."

"Axel. Hell of a name."

"Folks call me Axe."

"Axel, you have made a bad mistake."

The kid stared at him, looking hard with those brown eyes. "You going to kill me?"

"We'll see," Hutto said. "I want you to go back over it all, one, two, three, and tell me just how you came to be breaking into that Jeep."

"I tell you, man, I was after the tape deck."

"One, two, three."

"Okay. One, I come here a couple times a week in tourist season because it's hid from the main road by them trees over there. Two, I look around for something with a good tape deck in it that looks easy to get into. Three, I see your Jeep has got a Mitsubishi deck in it. That's how come I'm there."

"And the rest."

"That's all. There ain't no more."

"You work alone?"

"Brother's sick."

"Too bad."

"Yeah, he'd have kicked your ass."

"Next time, maybe."

"You let me go, okay?"

"I don't know. Somehow it doesn't seem right."

"You'd kill somebody over a tape deck?"

"I've killed people for nothing at all. People I didn't even know. For less than nothing."

"You're a crazy bastard."

"You better be nice to me, and you better leave my mother out of this."

82

"Anything you say."

"Up," Hutto said, motioning with the pistol.

"Oh, man, what you doing this for?"

"Just shut up and get to your feet. But first take off your shoes and leave them here."

"These my good shoes, man."

"You want to die with your shoes on, or what?"

He took them off, placing them carefully together beside the creek. He wadded up his socks and stuffed them inside the shoes.

Hutto waved him across the creek. They went through the cold water, stepping on rocks where they could. The kid whimpered a little about the water and the sharp rocks. "Quiet," Hutto said, and the kid was silent.

They went cross-country, off-trail, walking a half mile mostly up hill, going over some small ridges. Hutto stopped walking at another creek which dashed down between two slopes. "Stand there," he said, motioning the kid into the water.

"Oh, man, what you doing?"

"I'm giving you a chance to stay alive. Just a chance."

"This water is cold."

"Tough luck."

"It's killing me."

"Nope. That's my job, remember?"

"You said you wouldn't."

"Okay, Axel, here's your chance to live. I want you to stand right where you are until you count to one thousand slowly, that is, if you know how to count that high. Then you just take a nice easy walk back to the parking area, and you can pick up your shoes and go your way."

"My feet are freezing."

"That's the price you pay."

"They're all cut up from the rocks."

"Axel, don't tell me your problems."

"I see you again, man, I'll pick out your eyeballs and feed 'em to you."

"Somehow I don't think so, Axel."

"Why don't you just kill me and get it over with?"

"I take pity on the weak."

"I ain't weak."

"What are you, then?"

"I'm just broke, is all. I'm confused."

"You're weak. You're too weak for me to bother killing you."

"You're a weirdo, man. You're an el freako."

"Watch your mouth, Axel. When you see me at the top of that ridge over there, start counting. And if I see you or hear you behind me, you're done for. You're a goner. Understood?"

"I guess."

"Don't guess. Understood?"

"Yeah."

"And if I ever see you again, period, you're as good as dead. Right?"

"Whatever you say."

"I'd get out of the tape deck business if I were you, Axel."

"You ain't me."

"Somebody else is going to catch you someday, and they won't be as nice to you as I've been."

"Someday you'll pick on the wrong guy, big man."

"I doubt it."

Axel's face was bleeding in several places. His upper lip was raw and still dripping, and the skin around his eyes and forehead was already turning purple. His eyes followed Hutto's movements, and he turned his head to watch him go.

"You'll pay for this," he said.

"Bye-bye, Axel."

"You'll die."

"Not for a while. Don't forget to count, now."

Hutto moved quickly through the woods and along the creek, following it to the parking lot, and found Elizabeth sitting on the hood of the Jeep.

"What in the world?" she asked.

"We just had a friendly talk."

"Who was he?"

"Just your local tape deck thief."

"Did you kill him?"

"Not quite. He'll be sore for a while."

"Like everybody else around here."

She had moved both packs into the Jeep and was eating an apple. He wondered where it had come from.

"Let's go," he said.

"Where to now?"

"Now we do it all again."

"Oh, brother."

"By now you ought to be getting the hang of it."

"Couldn't we take the rest of the day off?"

"Haven't we had this conversation before?"

"Okay. Forget it."

She started the Jeep. He pointed right out of the parking lot, and she drove back toward Gatlinburg, elevation dropping fast. He looked out the window for something, a woodchuck, a deer, even a bear, but found nothing.

What a day, he thought. What a life.

## Chapter Eight

They went up a side road toward the ski lodge, winding away from Gatlinburg. He wanted to find a place to put the stuff, a place where nosy maids and plumbers wouldn't stumble across it. They bumped through some foothills, passing summer cottages, until he stopped at a complex with a sign out front reading, Chalet Rental.

The building looked like a worn-out country club. It had a swimming pool to the side and some tennis courts with grass growing through cracks in the cement. A half-dozen kids were by the pool, arguing about something.

The clerk inside was delighted to rent them a chalet. Hutto paid $300 cash for three days. Eric Connell sounded like a good name, so he signed it in the register. The clerk handed him a printed sheet of rules and regulations, said they were welcome to use the pool, courts, or Ping-Pong tables, if they wanted, and sent them on their way.

The chalet sat by itself on a point of land sticking off the hillside. He took a look around before going in. Gatlinburg reposed in the distance, quiet and insignificant from here. Birds sang in the trees. A squirrel sat on a stump, concentrating on a hickory nut. The place looked a little run-down, but it could be a slice of heaven in the wilderness, if it was just you and a woman, and you had nothing to do but explore each other. But it would be hell on earth if you had to defend it. You couldn't protect it from approach on any side, not if you were alone with a female who couldn't shoot.

They went inside. It was clean, neat, and spare. A folded typed note standing on the kitchen counter read, "Thank you for staying with us. We're very proud of our little mountain home and hope you treat it with the love we do. We have provided towels, linens, and all you need for your stay, and hope you leave everything for our next guests to enjoy." The note was signed, Bob and Tanya Chandler.

Bob and Tanya had fairly decent taste. Except for a picture of a crying clown in the bathroom, Hutto could find nothing that truly disgusted him. Elizabeth seemed to like it. She stood on the outside deck looking at the view.

"Nice place," she said when she came inside.

"And no maid service until we check out."

"What I need is a bath."

"No time," he said.

"I'm so sore I can hardly move."

"You weren't sore hiking because you were working your muscles. Now you're sore because you've been sitting in the Jeep."

"Carrying sixty pounds didn't help any."

"Women gain sixty pounds all the time when they're

pregnant."

"That's different."

"How? Sixty pounds is sixty pounds."

"Yeah, but when you're pregnant you put on a little at a time, until it all adds up to sixty. You don't just throw it on all at once."

"You sound like an expert."

"I am."

They stared at each other. He let the obvious question go unasked. "Let's go," he said. "It's getting late."

He didn't like leaving the cocaine anywhere, but felt better with it in the chalet, not open to view in the back of the Jeep for any thief who happened to bumble along. They drove on the same road they'd just come down, back uphill, following the west prong of the Little Pigeon River into the mountains, past the Chimney Tops, and the Alum Cave parking area. Hutto looked for Axel, thinking he might have made it out of the woods by now if he had remembered how to count. But he wasn't visible.

At a curve in the road he saw a woodchuck standing on its rear legs fussing at something. He liked woodchucks. Some people thought they were just big rats, but he figured they were little bears, and they were, in fact, closely related to bears. That's why they sleep the winters away.

He'd nearly had a wreck at this same curve in the road a couple of winters ago. A woman that interested him had wanted to go to the mountains despite snow warnings. It was warm in Knoxville, she reasoned. Why not the Smokies, too? But there was a twenty-degree temperature difference, and when the elevation increased, the flakes came down, and by the time they got this far, the road was iced. A car in front of them slid off the road. When he cut the steering wheel to avoid it, his car began to skate and turned around twice in the road.

The crazy woman wanted to go on. He headed back to town. She complained the whole time about not getting to go to the top. She said this snow was nothing compared to some she'd seen in the Rockies and those hadn't stopped her. He dropped her off at her house and never took her out again. His interest didn't extend to killing himself for nothing.

He looked at Elizabeth. She had her eyes closed, dozing in the sunlight as he drove. Mount Mingus came up on their right. Behind it lay Sugarland Mountain, but it couldn't be seen from here. To the left was Anakeesta Ridge. Anakeesta was a Cherokee word meaning balsam tree spot, or something like that.

The Cherokees had traveled all through the Smokies, leaving a name here and there to remember them by, but they had mostly lived in the foothills and lowlands. The mountains were sacred to them, and dangerous. They believed strange little troll-like people lived in caves here, and they didn't like to cross them.

Hutto thought the Cherokees were right. The mountains were dangerous, even if you knew them well. And they were certainly sacred, if anything is. For all he knew, there might even be some trolls hanging around, too.

The road wound up to Newfound Gap. This was the main pass where the highway dipped toward Cherokee, North Carolina. Stand in the right spot here, and you can put one foot in Tennessee and the other in North Carolina. There was a large parking lot here to accommodate the many tourists who wanted to stop and look out where the mountains dropped swiftly away, following the little Oconoluftee River as it fell to the foot of Richland Mountain and Hughes Ridge. Beyond there, the mountains called the Blue Ridge began, running hard northward.

Elizabeth eased out of the Jeep and stood looking at the view, which was beginning to cloud over.

"Where to now?" she asked.

"The Boulevard."

"What's the Boulevard?"

"Another trail."

"Where does it go?"

"You're not going to believe this, but it goes back up Mount Le Conte."

"Not again."

"Again."

"Twice in one day."

"We'll do it until we get it right."

"I don't know if I can. I'm not complaining. I just really don't know if I can do it."

"This is an easy trail."

"Sure."

"Really."

"Sure. They're all easy for you."

"There's not much elevation climb at all. It's a nice trail. Great views. You'll like it."

He helped put on her backpack, then started up the trail, leaving the crowded parking area behind. There was a rock overlook with a group of tourists lounging on it, and a rock-covered restroom with a dozen more hanging around there. Several were along the edge of the parking lot staring at the view or arguing with the children. He wanted to get away from there fast. Half those people could be deputies for all he knew.

"Thought you said this was flat," she said, lagging behind.

"It'll flatten out soon. Actually, it's not exactly flat. It's just less climbing than the other trails to the top."

"Actually, it's about to kill me," she said.

They passed two groups of people going the other way, down to Newfound Gap. One was friendly. The other averted their eyes, looking at their feet. Hutto wondered if that last bunch was cops trying to be undercover.

After two and a half miles, Hutto stopped and pulled out his Klecko, pointing it to his right down a barely visible trail.

"There already?" Elizabeth asked.

"Some is down there somewhere. We'll get it later."

"Why later?"

"Because it's going to get dark before too long and that's a tough place to work in."

"Why's that?"

"It's called the Jumpoff. That give you any idea?"

"Somehow the Boulevard sounds a lot better right now."

They walked on. The trail began to drop sharply through a big spruce forest.

"Thank God for some downhill," she said.

"What's downhill now is uphill coming back. And you'll be loaded."

"Thanks for reminding me."

They turned uphill again. Down to the left was Anakeesta Ridge, with its balsams, or Fraser firs. Then the path grew narrow and more spectacular. The ridge fell away on both sides, and they were walking on a steadier, safer version of Keyhole Ridge. They looked down on clouds, birds, trees, and it was a little like being a god, though a minor one, at best, striding swiftly along the heavens, observing mankind's meager efforts.

Then Hutto stopped, looked around to make sure they were alone, and consulted the Klecko, finding what he looked for. "It's down there," he said. "Let's go."

"Looks dangerous," she said.

"It is."

"Let me catch my breath."

"Look, the stuff is down there, and it's getting later and later in the day. We can't wait around long."

"This is a real strange-looking place down there," she said.

"They call it Huggins Hell."

"Why's that?"

"Beats me. It had to have a name, I guess."

"Sounds scary."

"Would you feel better if it was named Bambi Overlook or something?"

"I'll feel better when we're out of here."

"That's two of us."

The descent off the trail was steep and treacherous. Without the treasure somewhere below, Hutto would never have attempted it. He wasn't certain they could make it back up this way with full packs. Vines, rocks, and holes tripped them. Elizabeth kept her feet, but Hutto stumbled on something and rolled twenty feet, landing hard.

If he broke a leg here, he'd never get out. Elizabeth wouldn't be able to carry him. He'd have to lie here until the birds plucked out his eyes.

The Klecko was still in good shape despite the fall. It pointed him even further downhill, so they struggled through the growth, and went down and down, further than seemed possible, until he saw the deflated parachute caught on some brush.

They worked fast packing the load away, and after a few gulps of water, were ready to go. Uphill was murder. They tried it using their hands for claws and feet for hooks to keep from sliding backwards. He let Elizabeth use the goatskin gloves to save her fingers. His own were slashed from the rocks and briars. The heavy packs made it impossible. They couldn't do it, couldn't do it.

Until they did it, reaching the top exhausted. They both sat in the trail, watching Huggins Hell fade below them in the dying sunlight. Elizabeth appeared to be in pain. He touched her face.

"I'm all right," she said.

He slowly got to his knees, then to his feet. After a few minutes, he pulled her up, too. "I'm going to rename this place," he said. "From now on, it's Hutto's Hell."

Then a voice came from nowhere, a voice touched with irony, a voice seeming to rise from the Hell itself, a voice somehow familiar.

"Hutto's Hell is a right good name for it, if that's you'uns name," it said.

The man speaking stood twenty yards away down

the trail. He had a full graying black beard, long matching hair, and a flop hat on his head. He wore a flannel shirt, patched jeans, and combat boots. While Hutto watched, he spit a stream of tobacco juice between a gap in his upper front teeth.

Behind him, trying to look mean, was Axel, the tape deck specialist. His face was a mess, worse than Hutto remembered, and he wondered if somebody had further rearranged it after he finished with him. Two others, younger versions of the long-haired man in front, stood behind Axel.

"Hello, Axel. You a hiker, too?" Hutto said.

"We been looking for you," Axel said. "Seen your Jeep."

"Shut up," the older man said.

"Axel and I had a small disagreement this afternoon," Hutto said.

"Quit talking, little man," he said, shaking his long hair back. "You think you're a big man. You ain't nothing but small stuff."

"We'll find out."

"You look like small stuff, and the lady looks like good stuff. I didn't know there was a woman involved."

"She's not."

"You lie, little man."

Axel laughed. The other two shifted nervously behind him. Hutto could see no way out. He and Elizabeth couldn't possibly outrun them, not with heavy packs. He was sure they had guns, though he couldn't see any.

"Hutto's Hell," the older man said. "That's a good place for you to lay down your head if there ever was one."

The man crept slowly forward, keeping turned to his right side. Axel and the others eased behind him. Somewhere, Hutto had seen that walk, that snakelike slither, protecting an arm like a crosstie and, perhaps, a gun that would shatter this sunset quiet. Somewhere. Vietnam, maybe. Who could think? Who could think just now?

Not Hutto. He got ready to move.

People disappear in the Smokies all the time. Every summer, tourists go up a trail and never come down it. They're usually alone, or in pairs. They come from Ohio or Michigan or Ontario or Alabama, and they want a week of solace in the mountains, walking among ancient rocks, sniffing flowers they can't name. What they get is eternal quiet, with relatives throwing dead flowers atop empty graves.

The bodies are never found. Sure, there are some runaways, people who go to the Smokies for vacation, then wind up living under assumed names in Hawaii or Spain or Montana. But most who disappear have a good family and job or are engaged to be married. A surprising number are schoolteachers.

The search crews go out, the rescue squads, the National Guard, the local trackers with bloodhounds, and the Boy Scouts. They make a party of it, look around the mountains a week or so, camp out at night, tell old tales and play old tricks, but the missing person usually stays missing. They find no tracks, no signs, no notes scratched by a rock on a rock. Nothing.

The trails these missing ones walk are the same ones everybody else does. Their bootprints join with thousands of others. In every case, it seems they wouldn't have the nerve or bad sense to venture far from the trail. But they could. It's possible they may go off a ways, then fall in a hole made by a rotting tree stump. Their arms could be caught, trapped by their sides. They would struggle, scream, perhaps, once the initial embarrassment was over, then slowly die of thirst or hunger or exposure.

Wild boars could get them, too. That was another popular theory among the locals. Everybody knows wild boars are the meanest creatures in these mountains, introduced here years ago by a stupid rich man who brought them from Europe to stock a private game preserve. Of course, the preserve failed and the pigs got loose, and had been tearing up the woods ever since. You couldn't cross one; it would charge you for no reason, and those tusks could cut you apart quicker than an old cavalry saber. But you rarely saw one, unless you were looking hard and were far back off-trail at night. Yet the boars were the meanest animals here.

Except humans.

Few wanted to admit it, but crazy humans were far more likely than pigs to grab these wandering tourists. Somebody who knew the mountains well and understood the psychology of tourists could have been stuffing bodies in hiding places for years, and would never be caught.

Never, that is, unless the crazy ones picked the wrong tourist at the wrong time.

Hutto had always leaned toward the crazed human killer theory. Now he looked at the bearded man coming at him sideways, slowly, deliberately, step-by-step, and he saw hatred beyond reason in those eyes, hatred for the whole race of two-legged creatures, except those of his own seed and blood and place, and then Hutto knew this was the last thing those lost ones saw, those eyes, and that beard, and that ridiculous hat.

The man stopped. "Where's your gun at?" he asked.

"In the pack."

"Get it, Axe."

Axel limped up on his torn feet, now wearing his four-striped running shoes. "Sumbitch, you dead," he said, thrusting his face six inches from Hutto's.

"Left side pocket, Axel."

"You call me Axe."

"Somehow it doesn't fit, Axel."

The kid started to pop Hutto's face, but held back when the bearded man said, "Axe. Get a move on."

Axel undid the left side pocket and removed Hutto's pistol. He reached in again and withdrew the extra ammunition clips.

"Going for bear," Axel said. "This fool thinks he's going for bear."

The bearded man held out his hand and Axel put the gun in it. He turned it over, looking at it closely. "Too much noise," he said. "Prefer knives, myself."

He handed the pistol to one of the others, who put it in a daypack on his back. Hutto figured he was carrying water and food for the group.

Pulling a long knife from the sheath at his belt, the bearded man advanced on Hutto, sideways steps reminding Hutto of an Indian tracking a deer, or a bird dog approaching a covey of quail. He waved the knife in the air, flipping it from hand to hand, slicing at nothing.

Hutto got ready. He might be carrying an eighty-pound load, but he'd move, and move fast. The man grinned when he saw Hutto flex his fingers and get onto the balls of his feet. His beard was just long enough to flop from side to side as his head swayed in time to his steps. Hutto got set.

Then he was on the ground. The man charged when he was four feet away, and Hutto fell like his legs were cut from under him. He slid under the man, trying to take him down, too, but one combat boot caught him under the chin, and then the other, so that before he could recover, the knife was at his throat playing games with his Adam's apple, scratching it when he swallowed.

"What we got here, little man?" the man said. "What we got?"

Hutto lay there feeling the knife and thought about the throats he'd cut himself, mostly Oriental ones, and how the sinew and muscles tore, struggling, ripping, fighting. He remembered seeing the esophagus and how white it was, how innocent and vital, uncovered and severed. There was the time he delivered some cocaine in a sheep slaughterhouse, to the man who managed the place, and he'd gotten a tour of the kill line and had seen the same thing with the sheep, the clean, white, pureness of the trachea, and he knew his would look the same way.

He hated for Elizabeth to have to see it. He dreaded the humiliation, the embarrassment of being killed in such a way before her, of not being able to protect her from what would surely follow his death. He was ashamed for bringing her here in the first place, ashamed of his greediness, for not just being happy with the seventy pounds of stuff he'd parachuted with, for not taking it and Elizabeth and living happily forever in some foreign land where no one knew his name or his past, for not living his life free and alive and in a state of wonderment at the luxury, the simple gift of being on earth at this time, anytime at all, anyplace at all.

Then the man ground his face into the rock trail, scratching it, shaming him even more. He could feel the knife point fiddling away at his ear.

"What you got in the pack, little man? This is the heaviest pack I ever seen," the man said, keeping a knee on the back of Hutto's head.

"Just gear."

Then the knife came down to his nose, just off the ground, and the blade entered his left nostril, twitching there. He tried to hold his head as still as possible, feeling the delicate sharpness of the instrument.

"Gonna make you a new snot hole," the man said.

Elizabeth picked that time to make her move, charging the man while his back was to her as he concentrated on Hutto. She managed two steps before he heard her and whipped around, knife in hand, and stopped her cold with a slap across the face. She fell, awkward with the pack, and nearly slid off the Boulevard.

When the knife slipped out of his nose, it tore the lining off the inside of the nostril, so Hutto's lower face was flowing with blood when he turned to watch. By then, Elizabeth was already down, and the bearded man's three backups were on her, pinning her arms and legs.

They didn't need to. She was on her stomach, motionless, held there by the pack and exhaustion. Hutto watched the bearded man, who was still holding the knife, on his feet now, smiling. The daylight was nearly gone, and it was hard to see details. It was funny, but Hutto felt almost grateful to him for letting him live, for giving him a few more minutes. The man was a god of sorts. He could decree life or decree death, and it made no difference to him which was which.

He jabbed Hutto with the toe of his right boot, then turned and did the same with Elizabeth. "Time to get up, children," he said. "Time to go home and go to bed."

Hutto had a hard time getting to his feet. Elizabeth couldn't make it and was lifted up. Axel opened her backpack and removed one of the brown-wrapped packages inside. He tore the paper and sniffed at its contents.

"What's that?" he asked.

Elizabeth giggled.

"I asked you a question, girl," he said.

"Woman," she said.

"I asked you something."

The bearded one stepped across and took it from him, looking at it under the ever-brighter moonlight. He placed it carefully back in its place, then opened Hutto's pack and saw what was inside.

"You some kind of junkies?" he asked.

Elizabeth laughed.

"Shut your mouth, woman," he said.

He came around to Hutto's front, still holding the knife, and looked him directly in the eye. "Wipe your nose," he said. "You look like a little boy been in a fight."

Hutto cleaned off his face with his shirt. "How's that, sergeant?" he said

"Damn sight better."

"You can have it. Every gram," Hutto said. "We don't need it. You take it. Just let us go."

"What makes you think I want it? I ain't no junkie like you."

"Never touch the stuff, myself."

"Wait a minute," the bearded man said. "You with that guy in Pigeon Forge, that guy that fell out of the airplane in the middle of the night. You with him and that airplane that crashed up at Black Mountain. Cops looking everywhere for you, and here we done found you."

"What do you mean, they're looking everywhere for us?"

"Maybe not for you just exactly, but they're looking. Looking for something. They ain't been so worked up, ever. They say he had, what, seventy pounds of that stuff and it was worth $30 million bucks, something like that."

"Something like that. Depends on who you know. Cops like to inflate the dollars. Makes them look big."

"You got twice that much here, ain't you?"

"You can multiply, too."

"Boys, we looking at thirty million bucks times two, right here on top of Huggins Hell. Whoo-wee. We some rich sons of bitches now."

"Gotta sell it first."

"You telling me how to sell dope, little man? I come from a long line of moonshiners and bootleggers. But the glow is gone off that business, gone with the wind. Now that old whisky, that's nothing. We into grass now, marijuana, Miss Mary Jane. We got connections. We know people."

"You'll wind up in jail or dead if they're not the right people, though."

"People cross Riley, they never cross him again."

"Riley?"

"What about it?"

"Your name is Riley?"

"So?"

"So you and Axel must have been named by the same people. Old Riley and Axel. What a pair."

"I ain't that old," Riley said. "Axel here, he's my boy. He's got his problems. You seen that this afternoon. Make a fortune selling marijuana, and he wants to bust into cars and steal tape decks."

"And these two, they're your boys, too?"

"My sister's boys. Their daddy's dead and she's in prison over to Nashville. Killed her boyfriend. With a knife. They're good boys. They kind of help me out."

"How sweet," Hutto said.

"What are we going to do with you two?" Riley said. "What we going to do?"

"We could make a deal," Hutto said.

"I don't make deals."

One of the sister's boys, the one with long blond hair and a gray sweatshirt, started rubbing his hand on Elizabeth's arm. She slammed his face with her fist and he started after her.

"Cut it," Riley yelled, and the boy stopped. "Philip, don't you be a fool, too."

"Can I have her?" Philip asked.

"You'll get some," Riley said.

"She's so pretty."

"We'll all get some."

"This one's just right for me," Philip said.

"This one?" Hutto said.

"We do some hunting," Riley said.

"Hunting."

"Tourist harvesting."

"Harvesting."

"Dumb fools come up here where they got no business and act like idiots. Got full wallets, too, every one. We have a little fun with them and then put them out of their misery."

"Boy, you're a charmer, Riley. No wonder you're such a successful businessman."

"Shut your mouth, little man, and say your prayers. "You 'uns are next.

He shoved Hutto and Elizabeth further up the trail. Philip and Axel led the way. Riley and the boy called Judson came last. The backpack Hutto carried was agonizingly heavy. He wondered how Elizabeth could possibly carry hers. The trail itself wasn't terribly steep, and that's what saved them.

Hutto was sure he could climb no more, stumbling in the moonlight on the open trail, looking down on both sides seeing no lights, nothing, no movement, no people, no hope. He tried to put his mind on other things, cataloging the trees and plants they passed, the flowers hiding in the darkness by the rocks along the trail. The names were sweet on the tongue: mountain ash, parnassus, monkshood, gentian, myrtle.

At Myrtle Point, Philip and Axel stopped. Elizabeth sagged to the ground, and they let her lie there a moment. A creek fell away down the mountain on their left. Hutto tried to remember its name, thinking hard: Cannon Creek.

Then they dragged Elizabeth to her feet and the group turned off the Boulevard going down, down, down, to some rocky cliffs Hutto had never noticed before. Myrtle and rhododendron covered all the open space. Riley pushed them on through the undergrowth, impossibly thick, impossible to scramble through, but they did, with it catching their backpacks and pulling at their faces. They wound deeper, hitting a small canyonlike area, and then Philip and Axel disappeared, not ten feet ahead of Hutto.

He looked hard and could see nothing. Then Axel's head stuck out a narrow opening, looking stupid and mean, and motioned them in. Elizabeth moved forward, and Hutto followed, certain that something terrible was going to happen as soon as they entered that dark slit. Inside, he could see nothing. There was total blackness and the quiet shuffling sounds that accompany dark places in the forest. He heard the others breathing, then the sound of a match striking, and saw Riley light a kerosene lantern through the flare. Philip had his hand on Elizabeth's arm.

In the sudden light, she jumped back. "I thought it was you," she said to Hutto.

With the light, Hutto saw they were in a large cavelike opening in the bowels of the mountain. The floor had the ashes of many fires piled upon it, and the high roof of the cavern was black from catching the smoke.

He saw some bones and wondered if they were human.

He saw some humans and wondered how long it would be until they were bones.

## Chapter Nine

Riley and the others made themselves at home. Hutto saw piles of canned food and drink, carried in during many grueling hikes, and some rough chairs fashioned from split logs. They lit another lantern and started a fire with wood already cut and stacked against one wall of the cavern.

"Nice place," Hutto said.

"Better like it, little man. You be here a long, long time."

Riley told them to take off their backpacks and lean them against the wall.

"How much you got?" he asked.

"A hundred and forty pounds."

"Goes a long way, a gram at a time," Riley said.

Axel poked into the backpacks, scratching at what was within.

"Stay away from them things," Riley said.

"I just want to look," the kid said. "I ain't never seen nothing like that."

"Keep your nose out of there."

Axel backed away. Philip sat on a makeshift chair

and stared at Elizabeth. Judson pulled out a knife and began throwing it into the dirt at this feet.

Hutto's nose hurt. The inside of the damaged nostril was like a hog hide scraped clean. His Adam's apple quivered a little from its close call, and his ear had crusted blood on the lobe. He looked at Riley. Those crazy blue eyes, the unruly hair and beard, the long, lean torso and legs added to that menacing sideways approach to battle brought something to mind.

"You ever been to the Cavalcade Club on Kingston Pike in Knoxville?" Hutto asked.

"Cavalcade."

"Gambling in the back room. Girls, maybe, if you know what to say. A country band. It's closed now."

"You been there?"

"Yeah, I've been there."

"What you hang around them places for?"

"For the wonderful people you meet."

"Cavalcade. Why you ask?"

"I was just remembering a fight I saw there once. Out in the parking lot. This big guy took another guy apart. That guy never knew what happened, it was over so quick. He hit him with some sort of homemade karate, looked like. A couple kicks, a couple jabs, and it was over. That big guy came up on him sideways, like you do. He had a beard and hair kind of like yours. Of course, it was dark. Could have been somebody else."

"Whatever happened to that guy, anyway?"

"The loser? I didn't know him too well, but last I

heard, he was still crippled up, and that happened a couple of years ago."

"Little bastard. He deserved it."

"What did he do, anyhow?"

"Don't remember. Got in my way. Something to do with some old girl. He just got me riled."

"You could have killed him."

"I meant to."

"Now, if you had killed him, you'd be down at Brushy Mountain singing the jailhouse rock, and we'd be going merrily on our way."

"Cops can't touch me," Riley said.

"Why not?"

"Scared of me, that's why. Too smart for 'em."

"Riley, you're dumber than you think. Everybody makes a dumb move sometime."

Riley stared at Hutto through the flickering lantern light. He pulled a tobacco pouch from a rear pocket and stuffed a wad inside his cheek.

"You talk a lot for a little man fixing to die," he said.

"You won't kill us."

"Why not? What makes you a special son of a bitch?"

"Because you're not satisfied with 140 pounds of coke. You want it all, every gram of it. And we're the only ones who know how to find it."

"There's more?"

"Lots more."

"Where?"

"All over these mountains."

"It's here, me and the boys can find it."

"Not this. You'll never find this stuff."

"What'd you do, drop it out of that airplane?"

"What we did is our business."

"You'll talk."

"Not unless it's our ticket out of here."

"If that woman screams enough, you'll talk. We got our ways. We ain't dumb hicks, you know. The dumb hick business is over and done with. That's just something for the tourists to read on their menus at the restaurants in Gatlinburg."

"We talk, we walk."

"You ain't walking nowhere, not after you been here and seen this place. Give it up, little man."

Hutto leaned back, resting against his pack.

"I don't think so, Riley."

"We gonna see."

"Let's see, then."

Riley sat down next to Axel and opened up a can of Vienna sausages. He gulped a couple down, then drank from a paper package of apple juice.

"Want a weenie?" he asked.

"No, thanks."

"How about you, sweetie?" he asked Elizabeth. "Want a weenie?"

She just turned her head away, looking out into the darkness.

They sat there, listening to the slurping mouths sucking in weenies and beans and whatever else they had in those cans. Hutto wondered if this was a ritual of sorts, if they always sat eating while they watched their victims slowly give up all thought of living. He looked at Elizabeth, and she smiled at him, a small, frightened smile, but even at that, it made him feel better. He nodded at her and winked. That wink was supposed to say, it's okay, I'm in control.

"So what do you do with them?" he asked Riley.

"Who?"

"The bodies. The tourists you harvest."

"Bury them. Must be a couple dozen here in this cave. And maybe thirty, forty more in other places down the trail.

"Thirty, forty more?"

"Something like that. We keep busy."

"You're one sick person, Riley."

"Naw," Riley said. "I'm just your basic happy-go-lucky kind of guy."

"You've killed fifty people up here?"

"Forty, fifty, sixty. I don't know. Who counts?"

"Why?"

"They didn't have no business being here in the first place. This is my territory. Always has been. They was all lost souls, every one of them. Didn't know what they was here for, just taking up space, breathing my air. They all had money, which I could use. I'm not as broke now as I used to be, but money's still money. And the women, well, a woman's just a woman. I see one I want, I take her. That's that."

"You've never been close to getting caught?"

"Not once."

"But all the search parties, the dogs, the helicopters, they never bothered you?"

"Hell, no. It ain't no trouble outsmarting them fools. We usually join right in and search with them. Funny thing is, I bet half these people are never searched for. Never missed. Nobody cares. Folks must just assume they done run off from home or something. That's America for you. Disappear and nobody gives a flip."

"So you've killed people up here that nobody even knows anything about."

"Lots of 'em."

"Unbelievable."

"Know what?" Riley said.

"What's that?"

"I know two more going to disappear real soon. People back home will just assume they must have run off, must have been criminals, must have been escaping the IRS or the FBI or the CIA or something. Nobody will say old Riley got them."

"Wrongo, Riley. Wrongo."

"You think some cops gonna catch me?"

"No, Riley. I don't think some cop is going to get the chance."

"You ain't gonna stop me, little man. You gonna tell me where your coke is at, then you gonna go to sleep."

Axel laughed. He spit up some tobacco juice. "He'll eat your heart out, sucker," he said.

"He'll what?"

Philip rose from his chair, walking toward Elizabeth. "Their hearts. He eats their hearts," he said.

"You eat their hearts?"

"Makes me strong," Riley said. "Nothing like eating heart to give you strength."

"Something else I want to eat," Philip said, looking down at Elizabeth.

"Anybody messes with her, *I* do," Riley said. "I always go first."

"You ruin them," Philip said. "By the time I get them, they're all mashed up."

"You do what I tell you, boy."

"Let me get this straight," Hutto said. "You cut out their hearts and eat them?"

"While they're still beating."

"I want me some coke," Philip said. "Ain't never had nothing like that."

"You ain't going to, neither," Riley said. "Stay out of that pack."

"You such a big man, you make me."

"You're a cannibal," Hutto said.

"Ain't no cannibal. Don't go getting the wrong idea. What I am is a warrior. Indians ate their enemies' hearts sometimes."

"You're crazy," Hutto said.

"Such a big man. Damn big man," Philip said. He reached into Elizabeth's pack, quickly tore the wrapping off a brick of coke, pinched a huge amount between two fingers and stuffed it up his nose, sniff-

113

ing and snuffling.

"God damn you," Riley shouted, going at Philip in his sideways crab walk. "You ain't half the man your mama intended you to be. You ain't even half of Axe. You a fool, little boy."

"Whip your ass," Philip said. "Whoo. This stuff is good stuff." He crammed some more up his nose.

Riley was on him, then, kicking with those combat boots. One foot caught Philip flush in the nose, splattering blood and powder everywhere, and the other jammed him in the chest. Philip crashed to the floor of the cavern, but before Riley could pounce on him, his brother Judson had scrambled up and was throwing his knife at Riley. It caught the big man in the lower back, somewhere around the kidneys.

That was when Hutto moved, grabbing the second pistol they somehow hadn't found in the pocket of his pack, firing at Axel, who was scratching at Judson. The shot took off the back of his head and he dropped. Then Judson drew another knife and got set to flip it at Hutto, so he shot him, too, square in the chest. The noise, deafeningly loud in the cave, bounced off the walls and roof.

Hutto turned on Philip. "He's had enough coke to kill him," Elizabeth said.

"I guess I won't waste a bullet, then."

"I'll waste it," she said, and took the pistol from his hand.

"There's no need."

"I want to do it."

"He'll die anyway."

"I want to be sure."

She put the barrel of the pistol in Philip's ear. His eyes flared white all around their blue core and he struggled to speak, but couldn't get out a word. Hutto thought he would always remember that look in Philip's eyes, still bright and alive, and, after she pulled the trigger, fading, fading, until they were blank, nothing, just two marbles.

When Riley stirred behind them, she turned and fired at him, hitting him in the back. His blood splattered against the wall of the cave, and he lay still, with Judson's knife sticking out of his back.

Hutto slumped down in one of the homemade chairs. Elizabeth stood there still holding the pistol. He watched her, not entirely sure she wouldn't turn and fire it at him, too.

"Good shooting, Annie Oakley," he said.

"I don't know what happened to me."

"It's called adrenaline. Fight or flee syndrome. When it's pumping, you can't turn it off."

"Those bastards. They deserved to die. Every one of them."

"You're right about that."

"Gonna eat our hearts. Bastards."

Then Riley moved again, moaning a little. She whipped the pistol up and pumped another bullet into him. He flopped onto his back, tearing the knife from his muscle. His belly had a couple of large holes blown through the flannel shirt.

"Damn him, he won't die," she said.

"Maybe that's what comes from eating hearts."

She stood over Riley, pointing the pistol at his head. "Die, you son of a bitch," she said.

"I think he's a goner."

"You're so smart, you got us into this mess."

"At least I carried two pistols. They never thought about the second one. The moral of the story is, never go out with just one weapon."

"I don't think I can take any humor right now."

"Let's look around this place."

"Cannibals."

They took a lantern, dangling it at arm's length, walking back into the depths of the cavern. He saw it wasn't a big cave, that it didn't interconnect with the others sprawling beneath the surface of the mountains. The graves were hurriedly dug things, scooped out with a small shovel which still leaned against the side of the cave. The dirt was humped over them in small piles. On the floor of the cave, someone had taken a knife and drawn symbols that Hutto couldn't decipher. Some looked like letters, but weren't. Others looked a little like drawings of animals, but weren't.

"Devil worship," Elizabeth said.

"Maybe. Probably more like Riley worship."

"Riley was the devil."

"You can see it that way."

"He was. The others were junior devils."

On the side of the cave, above the shovel, were some names, most likely carved with a knife, all in a more-or-less feminine hand. He looked them over: Suzanna, Washington Court House, Ohio; Bitsy, Memphis, Tenn.; Laura, Greenville, Miss.; Janet and Frances, Lexington, Ky.; Jenny, Clinton, Tenn.; Meg, Anderson, S.C.; Angie, Traverse City, Mich.; Cindy, Columbia, Ind.

There were more, but he couldn't read them. The roll call of the dead.

Of course, Riley had to keep a record of his victims, had to keep track of the hearts eaten, the women subdued and conquered, the lives ended on the whim of a hillbilly devil-god.

In some boxes stacked alongside the wall, Hutto found more knives, camping gear, the kind of pornographic magazines that made sane people want to throw up, canned food, and several sticks of dynamite.

He knew what he had to do. He took the dynamite and made a bomb of sorts using what was at hand, the kind the Army taught him to make so many years before. It had a short fuse, just long enough to allow him to get away. Elizabeth watched every move he made.

"How'd you know to do that?" she asked.

He looked up at her, grinning.

"Don't tell me. Uncle Sam," she said.

He kept at it until he had it the way he wanted it. Then he carried it into the main room of the cave. Elizabeth walked in front of him with the lantern. She gave a little scream turning the corner and he came up next to her, fast.

"I can't believe it," she said.

He looked. Riley was sitting up, trying to stop the flow of blood from his stomach. It was more a river than a flow, an ocean of red goo, so he wasn't having much luck.

"Should have bled dry by now," Hutto said.

"He won't die."

"Everything dies."

"Not Riley. Not the devil."

"You wait and see," he said.

He took the pistol she carried and walked up to Riley, who was moving in slow motion, rubbing his wounds, moaning.

"Riley," he said. "Good-bye, Riley."

The big man tried to move away but couldn't get his legs working. "Little man," Riley said, struggling with the words. "Little man, you done it."

"No, Riley, the world did it. Suzana and Jenny and Meg and Cindy and all the other ones did it. Good-bye, Riley."

He put the muzzle between Riley's eyebrows and pulled the trigger. The shot slammed the big man's head back onto the dirt floor. He flopped once and settled.

Then Hutto and Elizabeth took the backpacks outside the cave a safe distance. She waited while he returned to the cave, found the pistol Axel had taken from him, stuck it in the waistband of his pants, and placed the dynamite bomb in the center of what was left of Riley's stomach. He took a small branch from the burning fire, lit the fuse, then ran outside. A few seconds later, he and Elizabeth, standing together by the packs, heard a thump, and then the ground shook.

When Hutto looked again into the opening, it was completely filled with rock. Nobody would ever go in there again. The roll call of the dead had ended, he thought, but add four more names.

## Chapter Ten

She put her arms around his neck. They stood together in silence among the myrtle and rhododendron, lost among the undergrowth in the moonlight. She stirred a little, and he felt her lips nibble the soft spot behind his ear.

"What time is it?"

"Midnight," he said.

"Two days. Seems like we've been doing this half our lives."

"It's a new day now."

"A new day and all is swell."

"Well, a new day, anyhow."

"That was nearly half a lifetime in there with Riley," she said.

"He's gone now."

"You sure?"

"Positive."

"Damn cannibal wouldn't die."

"He's dead now."

Hutto felt drained. He wasn't sure he could hike out of here, not even downhill. Killing steals life from the killer, he thought, even if the dead ones deserve to die. A human goes from thriving muscle to mouldering flesh in a blast of noise and tumult, and on to dust with the passing days, while the killer walks about with a little part of him numb, dead, gone. Hutto suspected even Riley felt this, and perhaps eating hearts was a way to hold off the feeling.

Elizabeth's fingers tugged on the hair at the back of his head and entwined there. He let her play for a minute. They might have been lovers out for a moonlit walk among the wild beauty of the mountains. But he couldn't push away the thought of the cave, now filled forever, and what rested within it, Riley and the boys, and all the Carolyns and Judys and Megs and Suzannas.

"We better go," he said.

"Things to do, places to be."

"Right."

"Coke to smoke."

"Not hardly," he said.

They put on the packs, first drinking some water, and wound through the brush thicket trying to pick up the faint trail they'd come on. He couldn't find it, but in their wanderings came upon a rocky point above an abrupt cliff, and from there he saw the shape of the mountain above, and could plot a path to take them back to the Boulevard. He might have tried to go straight downhill, back-country, had Elizabeth not been there.

If a back-country park ranger should happen to

stumble across them in the middle of nowhere with huge, heavy packs, he'd know something was wrong. Riley had said the cops were looking for something, somebody, somewhere. Hutto planned to not give them a clue. They'd stick to the main trails with the tourists and long-distance hikers. With packs like these, they'd look like they were walking the Appalachian Trail from Maine to Georgia, something lots of people did every summer.

The climb went slowly. Footing was uncertain and the undergrowth fought them every step. They both slipped and fell whenever they got going good. Hutto slid into some sort of sticker bush and got thorns in his arms and legs. Elizabeth scraped the skin on her arms. Twice they came to dead ends, cliffs they couldn't hope to overcome with loaded packs in the dark. It was two in the morning when they finally reached the top, about a quarter mile from Myrtle Point, where Riley had led them down to his own private hell.

Elizabeth lay face down in the trail, breathing softly. The big pack on her back made her look like a turtle, a turtle that had given up crossing the road and was begging the cars to hit it.

Hutto was afraid if he lay down, he wouldn't be able to get up, and they'd still be there at sunrise when the more energetic hikers from the shelter on top of the mountain would be hustling down the trail. He stood there, hands on hips, balancing the heavy pack, looking at the stars overhead.

From here, with no city lights to wash them out, they looked close and inviting. He could see Orion and the Dippers and some others whose names he had forgotten, glowing sketches of dogs and goats and people in the sky. If he could have gone back and redone his life, he wouldn't have minded being an astronaut, flying around out there looking at things, a little bit closer to the stars. He wouldn't have minded at all, but while he was reliving life, he'd have to do better at mathematics and some other school courses, and have a better attitude in the military.

He gave her fifteen minutes to rest, looking at the heavens' free show all the while, then shook her shoulder.

"What?" she said.

"Gotta go."

"Riley?"

"Dead and gone."

"You scared me."

"Sorry."

"I was asleep."

"I noticed."

She got to her knees, swaying under her load, ate a couple of peanut butter crackers he gave her, and drank some water.

"Easy on the water," he said. "We're low."

She finished up and struggled to her feet. He held out a hand for her but she ignored him.

"I guess you were shocked down there by what I

did," she said.

"I was just a little surprised. You didn't have to plug them like you did."

"But I did. I had to know they were dead. I had to know myself. I couldn't have lived in a world where they were alive and running around hurting people."

"It's okay. It's no big deal. Forget it."

"I can't."

"It'll go away in time."

"I'm like those Indian women that cut up the bodies of their enemies after a battle. I guess I went crazy for awhile."

"Don't worry about it."

"The worst thing is, it feels good. Does it make you feel that way?"

"Sort of clean and fresh? No," he said, and led the way down the Boulevard. The trail, under the bright moon, was easy to follow, but tired as they were, they still tripped on the rocks. When they came to the part of the trail where the mountain dropped away on both sides, Hutto worried about Elizabeth flipping over the crest. A fall there could go unbroken for hundreds of feet. She'd roll down the steep slope, unable to stop herself, and the big pack would break her back, just like Wilson's had broken his.

He thought about tying them together with climbing rope, so if she fell, he could at least brace her and maybe pull her back to safety. But if someone saw them, someone who knew anything about the mountains, that would definitely look odd. Odd enough to take a closer look.

So they made their way separately, neither one talking much, and in two hours had gone all the way down the Boulevard, connecting with the Appalachian Trail. Not long after that, going mostly downhill, they walked back onto the asphalt of the Newfound Gap parking lot.

Their Jeep and five other vehicles were there. Two were big land-cruiser-type mobile homes, with the owners undoubtedly asleep inside. In a Chevrolet, he saw a young couple sleeping in the back seat, the girl with her hand inside the boy's shirt. A Volkswagen bus sat empty. And the last vehicle, an old Buick with cans, bottles, and candy wrappers covering the floorboards, must have belonged to Riley and the boys. He opened the driver's side door and took a look. Two big knives were under the front seat and a pistol was in the glove compartment. If Riley preferred knives, somebody else obviously took a shine to pistols. Axel, probably. Luckily, he'd left it here.

They met no cars on their drive down the mountain.

"Think anybody will miss them?" she asked.

"Riley and Axel and the wild bunch?"

"Yeah. Think anybody will pine away wondering what happened to them?"

"Maybe. Could be a mama snake misses her babies once they're gone."

"Nobody missed those others in there, the Suzannas and Karens and the others in the graves."

"They might have been missed."

"Not enough to find them. Some of them weren't even looked for. You heard what Riley said."

"Because you're gone, doesn't mean you're not missed. There are so many runaways now and so many unhappy people, I guess their folks just assumed they had moved to a beach in Florida or to Las Vegas or California. Half the country runs off to California at one time or another, even schoolteachers and lawyers and secretaries."

"If I loved somebody and that person disappeared, I'd find out what happened," she said.

"How?"

"I'd just do it, even if it took forever. I'd find out."

"How would you know where to start?"

"I'd find out. Lots of times runaways just want somebody to show they love them enough to find them. Runaways aren't always running from something. Sometimes they're running to something."

"You sound like an expert again," he said.

"I am."

"Want to tell me about it?"

"I'm too tired. Anyway, it's a dull story."

"Try me."

In the glow of the dashboard lights, she looked soft, full of grace. She chewed her lower lip and tapped a finger on the armrest. He looked at her and saw a different woman than the one he used to see with Wilson. That woman was sometimes sullen, perhaps even on occasion mean, with a quick retort for everything. Her only real interest back then seemed to be drugs, and she mentioned cocaine at every possible break in the conversation. He remembered her laugh, controlled, cold, ready to hurt. She had looked hard sometimes back then, with sharp edges.

Now, after two days in the mountains, two days spitting in the eye of death, she looked softer, rounder, more of a woman. Even though she had been carrying a mountain of cocaine on her back, she rarely mentioned it other than to curse its weight. He hadn't heard her laugh all day. Maybe it was Wilson who had brought out the worst in her, he thought. Maybe his death and this struggle had set her free.

"You don't want to hear it," she said.

"I have a shoulder to cry on."

"Yeah, and a pillow to lie on, like the song says."

"That, too, if it comes to it."

"There are a million stupid stories just like mine."

"That doesn't make it less important."

"Okay, you asked for it. I'm from a little place in north Alabama, close to a town you probably never heard of called Gadsden. Strictly middle of nowhere. My father worked in a Goodyear tire plant. My mom didn't do much of anything except go to church a lot. I went to school. Didn't try hard.

There was a lot of marijuana around, and beer. I got onto that and started hooting it up every chance I got. Then when I was sixteen, I got pregnant by a boy who just laughed at me when I told him. I ran off to the interchange on I-59 and stuck out my thumb and this guy picked me up and the next thing I knew I was in Knoxville.

"I was so far along then I couldn't get an abortion, even if I'd wanted one, and that guy that gave me the ride wouldn't let me stay with him. So I hit the streets with that big belly sticking way out. Made a living any way I could. Went to one of those family aid agencies when it was time to have the baby, and said my folks were dead. So they helped me out a little bit, and took the baby and put it up for adoption. I never even saw it.

"After that, I got a job as a dancer in a strip joint. The Bare Cat. You been there, haven't you? I did that, working for tips, doing table dances naked as a baby for five bucks a song, clipping the customers for drinks when I could. I did a little dating on the side for pretty good money. Things were working out. I had a little bank account. I knew some people.

"I was there a long time. I saw some things you wouldn't believe. A lot of people are just animals, you know. I did some traveling. Worked in Memphis and Dallas and Atlanta, but always came back to Knoxville. Don't know exactly why, but I guess it seemed more like home, and it was closer to Alabama. I thought maybe sometime I'd be there doing something, and my daddy or somebody I knew would show up and take me back home.

"But that never happened. Then I met Wilson. He got me out of the life, away from the Bare Cat. Sometimes I go back there and those same girls are there, the ones who were dancing way back when I first started eight years ago. Some are still pretty good. Some got fat and are just waitresses now. Some just hang around waiting to get picked up. I didn't want to get like that.

"Wilson gave me things. Cars. Clothes. Money. Coke. I thought he needed me. I was making out fine. Kept thinking about showing up back in Alabama sometime in a big car and fancy clothes, but I never did it. Wilson could be mean, but he treated me good, at least compared to what I'd been used to.

"Now he's gone, too. I guess if I get out of this, I won't have to worry about any more Wilsons or taking my clothes off for a living, will I?"

"Nope."

"He wasn't going to take me with him, was he?"

"What do you mean?"

"When this little adventure you two had planned was over, he was going to dump me, wasn't he?"

"I think so."

"I was going to be stuck here to deal with the cops and the Colombians and the whole bit, for a measly million bucks, wasn't I?"

"I guess you would have been."

"You didn't try to say a word about that?"

"You were his girl, not mine."

"You could have stood up for me."

"I hardly even knew you. You were just the latest in a long line of Wilson's women. I didn't even want you in this. If we hadn't needed a driver, you wouldn't be here now."

"And miss out on all this fun?"

"It would have been a terrible thing to miss."

"I just can't imagine what I'd have been doing with myself."

"Wilson's funeral, maybe."

"I hope they cremate him and scatter him over the city sewage treatment plant."

"A sweetheart like Wilson?"

"He was waving a million dollars in front of my nose so I'd take the bait and let him get away. Can you believe that?"

"Only too well."

Hutto drove past the Sugarlands visitor center, into the edge of Gatlinburg, and up the road to the chalet. He parked a couple hundred yards away and walked through the woods to check it out. No one was there.

He didn't expect the cops to find it. But the Colombians . . . you can never tell about the Colombians. They might make the tussle with Riley look like a game. The Colombians didn't play games. When they looked at you and went bang-bang, you were dead. They didn't eat weenies with you and gloat over their conquests.

The Cowboys fired first and asked no questions at all.

## Chapter Eleven

When he woke, Hutto heard Elizabeth's soft breathing next to him. Her lips were slack, her mouth open, and her forehead was smudged with mountain soil. He watched a moment as the air huffed in and out, filling her lungs, then eased out of bed, slipped on his jeans, and walked to the balcony.

The sun was up, already hot, at ten o'clock. They should have been back up there, going for another grand prize package, but Elizabeth needed to sleep. Hell, I need to sleep, Hutto told himself.

Out in the forest just a few feet from where he stood, he saw a squirrel worrying with a nut, and some blue jays cursing each other in blue jay lingo. Must be nice to be a woods creature and not have any troubles, he thought. No problems except staying alive, the same thing every beast who ever drew breath had to worry about.

All staying alive meant was that you got another chance to reproduce yourself. That's the basic drive, that's everything right there. Somewhere deep inside every brain ticked a tiny clock that whispered go, go, go to the reproductive organs. If there's any immortality, it lies in that litany, that chant, the go, go, go at our core, the will to put another little Hutto or Elizabeth right here on two feet.

That's the secret of every singles' bar, and every slit-skirted woman and shirt-barely-buttoned man within them, the drive behind every singles' Sunday school class, and every teen dance. That's what the perfume makers knew long ago, and the car and soft-drink makers were now learning. People listened to that little voice. It made them do crazy things they said were out of character when they woke up in the morning and looked back at the night. But they couldn't help it. Despite the high thoughts and the pride of character, that little voice, that tiny clock, was what they were. Everything else was just pretty paper. It said go. They went.

After all those times following that little voice, Hutto had still not reproduced himself. Too many women, too many hard nights, too many bars and beaches and bashes, but still, in the most basic sense, he had failed to perform his duty. His blonde wife with the magnificent legs had made certain no seed he planted bore fruit, then after she divorced him, while he was in prison, she married a stockbroker and quickly produced a set of twin boys, and then another little blonde female creature who looked astonishingly like her mother.

He knew it was his fault. After all, he was the one in prison, not her. He had sprung that kid from jail, and he had just as surely been the one who killed him, even though he hadn't pulled the trigger. His motives were pure, straight out of a heroic myth, but his actions were tainted from the start. He saw it now. He couldn't blame his ex-wife. Why should she hang around a defrocked lawyer—even one from a well-to-do family—who could never set foot in her church again or play another round of golf at the club, or have a drink in certain partying establishments. She had gotten sympathy, at first. Then as his drug-smuggling money came in, and when it became clear that he was still dear to his department store-owning family, the old people and places indicated they were ready for him to repent and join again.

They felt there was nothing wrong with a certain kind of crime, only in getting caught. His crime, a crime of compassion, was the wrong kind, though. He'd done his prison time. Since he had money, they'd let him prove he was worthy. Their attitude was benevolent, forgiving.

Let them go to hell, he thought. They will anyway. Nearly everybody does.

The ex-wife was blameless, though she, too, would probably fry. He knew now she had been pushed and pulled by two different urges. The little voice inside her head, the tiny clock ticking away, had whispered go, go go. But the voice of society, the clock drilled into her by her friends and by magazines and books and television, shouted wait, wait, wait. But she wanted to find her purpose in life. She wanted to dream and scheme and party. Diapers were out of the picture.

Then when Hutto fell so hard, she saw some new wrinkles, some extra flab on her body, and maybe she felt tired, almost used-up. The stockbroker, listening to his own little voice, had been there when she finally heard hers and let it take over. No, she hadn't been wrong, exactly. She was just out of control, like so many people. Like Hutto himself.

Since he'd gotten out of prison, Hutto had urges he couldn't explain, things that seemed to have nothing to do with any little voice or tiny clock. He knew they did, somehow, but he couldn't figure how. He wanted more than this life could offer. He wanted adventure, something simple walks in the mountains couldn't provide. He wanted his own personal tango with death.

The usual run-of-the-Caribbean drug-smuggling business hadn't been enough for him. The money would have thrilled most men, and the danger would have been more than adequate. The Cocaine Cowboys should have been excitement enough, even on their average days when they weren't mad at you. But he had to cross them, had to beat them somehow, beat them out of enough money to die for a hundred times over. Now, Wilson, despite his looniness, had been listening to his little voice all along, because he was going to use his money to buy women and time for nothing but more women.

Hutto didn't want women. He'd had women. He wanted a woman. A woman soft and warm and loving to join him at the base of the Swiss Alps where they would do nothing but listen to the rhythm of their own hearts, and perhaps produce a little Hutto or two.

Out in the woods, not too far from where he stood on the balcony, Hutto heard a woodpecker's tap, tap, tap, and he saw it, following the staccato until he saw its red head pounding up and down, drilling deep into a dead hickory tree searching for a grub. What a way to live, beating your head against a tree, then flying on to another tree, and another, and on until you started to fly one time and flopped to the ground instead. The tap, tap, tap rolled on, insistent. He watched the bird until it crossed to the other side of the tree.

When he turned to go back inside, she was already up, standing at the sliding glass door, watching him. "Thinking about quitting?" she asked.

"Why do you say that?"

"That faraway look in your eyes."

"Just thinking. That's all."

"Well, what about it?"

"What about what?"

"I figure we've got 350 pounds of stuff, minus what Philip wasted. How many million dollars is that worth?"

"A lot," he said. "You know the story, though. We're not quitting."

"Mister Perfect. No loose ends, right? You're gonna do it your way, just because you say so, huh?"

"It's my way because I don't want to leave any clues. I don't want those Colombians to know where we are, or where we've been, or anything at all. I want them totally out of it."

"Are they that tough?"

"Tougher than tough."

"What's the deal? All they can do is kill us. How much deader than dead can you get?"

"I don't want to find out."

"What if they're here now?"

"You're certainly Miss Cheerful this morning."

"Midnight shootouts with cannibals do it for me every time."

He began getting their packs ready to go. They'd have to get more food before heading back up the mountain.

"Get dressed so we can move out," he said.

"But I'm serious. What if they're here?"

"Then we deal with them just like Riley and the boys."

"But they won't be that dumb, will they?"

"No, they won't. Bet on it."

They loaded the Jeep and set out again. In town, Hutto bought a newspaper, went inside a store and emerged with a bag of cheese, peanut butter crackers, sardines, and candy bars. He handed them to her through the open window with the newspaper.

"Wilson's famous," he said, and flipped the paper to the front page, which was half-covered with a story and photo about Wilson's exploits. Another story speculated about the crashed plane at Black Mountain and tried to tie it to Wilson. All in all, Wilson came across as a sharp guy working every angle. That was fine with Hutto.

He had changed a five-dollar bill for quarters at the store. He went to the phone booth outside it, talked for ten minutes, then made another call and talked ten more.

"What are you doing?" she asked when he came back to the Jeep.

"Making arrangements."

"You make it sound like a funeral."

"Don't be funny."

"Arrangements for what?" she asked.

"For you," he said. "I know this guy in Atlanta and he's going to help you get out of here."

"How's a guy from Atlanta going to get me out of here?"

"You'll just have to wait and see about that."

She scanned the story about Wilson as he drove the Jeep from the parking lot and back up the road entering the park.

"People must be wondering where we are," she said.

"Not me. I disappear all the time. Nobody knows where I am most of the time."

"But you're a known associate of Wilson's. Says so, right here in the paper. It calls you a disbarred lawyer with suspected ties to the drug underworld."

"Yeah, and you're a known associate, too."

"Wilson had a lot of known associates, female ones, particularly. You said yourself you hardly knew who I was."

"I didn't mean it that way."

"Yes, you did. He had all kinds of women. I wasn't the only one."

"The main one, though."

"For awhile. Not for long."

"Well, anyway, that's all over now."

The Jeep passed the park visitors' center, with its lot full of cars and campers.

"I'm sick of seeing this road. I'm sick of these mountains," she said.

"I wouldn't get so down on them. They're making you rich."

"No, *you're* making me rich."

"And look what it's getting me."

"What's that supposed to mean?"

"Nothing," he said.

"Sure, I bet."

"Look, I'm sorry. Let's don't fight until this is over."

The road followed the river, winding through the hills to Newfound Gap. The parking lot was half full of cars and campers, with families milling around everywhere. Some children were playing catch with a beach ball.

Hutto drove the Jeep the length of the lot, looking around. Then he parked. "Riley's car is gone," he said.

"Maybe it got towed."

"Not this fast."

"Maybe somebody stole it."

"That old heap?"

"There's got to be an explanation," she said.

"I'll bet the explanation is that somebody missed Riley and the boys and came here looking for their car. Whoever it was knew about the cave. When they found it filled up, they hiked back out here and took the car. They had to move fast. I bet they were here less than an hour ago."

"It was probably just sweet little old Mrs. Riley."

"She's too busy staying home sharpening knives."

They started up the trail, moving steadily. There were hikers everywhere, lots with little daypacks out for a mile-long leg stretcher, and a few with big packs like theirs, the serious hikers. These carried walking sticks like the one Hutto cut for Elizabeth the first day, and they took long smooth strides. The others, the ones who belonged in the cars back in the parking lot, took their time, meandering along poking at moss and ferns, sniffing the little purple flowers along the path.

The trail here, the same one they started out on yesterday, went up the slopes of Mount Kephart where the Boulevard went veering off to the left up

Mount Le Conte. Hutto always felt good about hiking to Mount Kephart just because of its name. Horace Kephart was Hutto's favorite of all the people associated with the history of these mountains. He came here because he chose to, not because he was born here, or because the government sent him, or to take a job, but simply because he wanted to.

Kephart grew up in the Midwest, took degrees from distinguished Eastern colleges, and became a librarian in St. Louis. He hated the work and dreamed of something bigger, became a drunk, then nearly died a broken man. Desperate for change, he left his wife and family in 1904, at forty-two, and wound up here, in the Smokies, because it was the closest wilderness available. He arrived in Dillsboro, North Carolina, on a train, hiked up into the woods as far as he thought he needed to go, found an abandoned cabin, and moved in.

He rested on the Little Fork of the Sugar Fork of Hazel Creek over on the North Carolina slope until he felt like living again. Then he got interested in the people of the mountains as well as the natural beauty. He learned how they lived, what concerned them, and their hopes and dreams and loves. Within two years he began to write, and he told the tale of these people as well as he could, in books read across this nation by those who could never travel here, and if they did, could never hope to see what Kephart saw.

When it became obvious that the timber companies would destroy Kephart's wilderness, he led the fight to make these hills into a national park. From 1920 on, it dominated his speech and his writing. People listened. In 1931, the largest timber company sold its holdings to the federal government. Less than a week later, Kephart was killed in a car wreck. Franklin Roosevelt dedicated the park in 1940, and Kephart's name went on this magnificent peak, Kephart the drunk, Kephart the dreamer.

At about 6,000 feet, on their way to the top of Mount Kephart, they came to the Smokies' little Canada again. The fir and spruce looked a lot like those in the mountains north of Vancouver. Hutto had gone there a time or two, on one sort of deal or another, and liked the dramatic change of those mountains. Skiing the slopes of Whistler was a world away from Gatlinburg.

But so was the 6,000-foot level of Mount Kephart. He saw some yellow birch and mountain ash. Even the birds here were different from those down below. He wasn't sure of their names, but could distinguish the coloring.

They plodded on another half mile, gasping a little in the thinner air, to a place where they could look across to a mountain called Charlie's Bunion. A rough tumble of rocks spread below them. She watched the scenery across the way while he consulted his Klecko.

"Are we there?" she asked.

"Welcome to The Jumpoff," he said.

Somewhere down there lay another 140 pounds of white powder, dearer to some people than gold.

## Chapter Twelve

The wind blowing up over the Jumpoff was cool and brisk, with some bite to it. Hutto wondered if he should have brought an extra shirt, or maybe a sweater. One time he'd been caught in a May snowstorm above the 6,000-foot level, and it was as bad as anything he'd ever been in. Of course, this wasn't May, and this wind carried no clouds.

They'd be out before dark if everything went right. But, if everything had been going right, he and Wilson would have been here already, collected their money, and gone their separate ways, one to the beach beauties, the other to the Alpine meadows. You can't count on things going right.

"What now?" Elizabeth asked, looking over the edge.

"Now we go down there."

"Where is it?"

"Somewhere down that way. That's all I know."

"Why couldn't any of it just land in the middle of the trail?"

"If it did, it'd be gone by now. Boy, those would be some happy hikers when they stumbled across that."

He didn't want to go straight over the Jumpoff, so he went through some brush looking for a better way, something with more slope to it. The undergrowth got thicker, so he stopped and checked his Klecko again, decided they were going too far away from the stuff, and eased back toward the edge. Finally he lay there a couple of feet from a mountain laurel and thought about it.

A little blackbird with a yellow bill flew onto the laurel and sat there looking at him, cocking its head from side to side. It looked like it was saying, "No, no, no."

He ignored it.

"Today we have to be careful," he said.

"What's so special about today?"

"By today half the world has had time to figure out where we are."

"But they haven't, I bet."

"I bet they have a pretty good idea."

From here, he could see a way down. It looked like a trail some animal used. Deer, maybe. Except deer usually didn't live this high. Humans, possibly. It didn't matter.

He pointed her down it, letting her go first since it wasn't too steep. Elizabeth held to the undergrowth and balanced back against the side of the mountain.

While he followed her, he looked behind to see if anything moved with them. Nothing was there. He tried to plan something if they were attacked, but could think of nothing particular to save them. You always need a plan. Without a plan, Grant would never have beaten Lee. Of course, Lee had a plan, too, if you wanted to look at it that way, and look what good it had done him.

What was his plan? Shoot the hell out of them, whoever they were? Then what? Run?

He couldn't work it out, so he let it go. Just think about the hike, think about the birds and trees and the little animals. Think about life.

They dropped lower and lower, following the Klecko's urging. She saw the parachute first, small and wadded against some rhododendron. Getting to it was tough. They had to climb some big rocks, going back uphill, then down the other side and through heavy undergrowth to get to the package.

When they finally got there, the chute was on the ground, but the coke wasn't. Some of the brown wrapping paper was scattered around the base of the brush, and the ground had a whitish appearance, brighter than the rest of the soil and grass in the area.

"Another bear?" Elizabeth asked.

"I think it did a Wilson on us."

"What?"

"I think we were too low when we dropped it. It must have hit before the chute got fully open, and the impact blew the pack apart. I'd say there was a cocaine explosion here."

"So we came down here for nothing?"

"Not for nothing," he said, and started digging a hole with his knife for the chute and the remains of the paper. "We get rid of this, there's that much less chance of getting caught."

They buried everything they could find and dropped the little tracking device, still doing its job despite the crash, into the hole with the rest of the disaster.

"Well, that was a zillion buck boom," he said when they were finished.

"Damn you and Wilson for your bright ideas," she said. "You could have just dropped all this stuff in my backyard, and nothing would have happened to it. By now we'd all three be cruising the islands."

"Is that your fantasy, cruising the islands?"

"I guess that's one of them. Why?"

"When people get access to a lot of money they have fantasies."

"What's wrong with that?"

"Not a thing."

"My life needs changing."

"Nothing wrong with that."

"People have to keep growing, you know."

"Okay, I agree with that."

"You don't have fantasies, I guess, since you're already so rich."

"Sure, I have fantasies," he said.

"Like what?"

"Well, I've already done the islands, so that's not my fantasy. I sort of wanted to go to the Swiss Alps and live in a quiet little village. I thought I could learn French better and teach myself German and read all the books I've been putting off. I could work on my skiing and maybe do a little mountaineering."

"You already had enough money to do that. You could have done that without ever touching a gram of coke."

"I guess."

"So why didn't you?"

"I don't know. Why do people always fail to carry out their fantasies?"

"Do they?"

"Yeah. You'd probably just go to the islands and develop an allergy to the sun or something."

"And you'd probably introduce the Swiss to the wonders of South American snow."

"No, I swear, I don't touch the stuff myself. And after this, I hope I never see another gram of it."

"And I'm not going to get allergic to the sun."

They started to work their way back up the slope. Hutto was glad the pack was light, because his thighs were working too hard as it was. The narrow animal trail they had followed at the top faded not too far from the Jumpoff, so they had to make their own way, going from clump to clump of brush.

He led, going slowly, making sure each foot got a firm hold before pushing on. Elizabeth grunted along behind him, cursing under her breath every now and then. He decided her curses were a kind of fuel to push her on, and he didn't mind them. Whatever she did, it was bound to be more acceptable than what Wilson would have done had he not taken the overloaded plunge into Pigeon Forge.

It wasn't that far to the top. In his prime he could have almost kicked a football that distance. But the difference between horizontal and vertical feet was enormous. Walk on level ground and you just skate along. Your weight is next to nothing. Go vertically and you lift your entire body weight with each step.

Stopping at a big rock with a spectacular view of Charlie's Bunion, Horseshoe Mountain, and what must be the even bigger Porters Mountain beyond it, he took off his pack, reaching for water and candy bars.

"Thought you were the one in such a big hurry," she said.

"I am. But we have to rest, or we'll never make it. Can't get too tired here. If we got hurt, we'd be in a mess."

"You'd just leave me?"

"No, I'd get you out somehow. Ten feet an hour if I had to."

"That's nice to know."

"But there's no way you could move me if I broke a

leg or something," he said.

"I'm stronger than I look."

"Not that strong."

"I'd get you out. Worst came to worst, I'd hike out for help."

"That kind of help would just put us behind bars."

"Better than being dead, isn't it?"

"Not for me. Better dead than rocking in the jailhouse."

"That's right. You ought to know a few choruses of that. Wilson told me."

"Two-years' worth."

"You were a bad boy?"

"I didn't think so. I was trying to right a wrong, and it just didn't work out."

"You were a lawyer. You ought to have known better."

"No more lawyering for me."

"How come?"

"A jury of my peers decided I wasn't fit to practice."

"Maybe in Switzerland."

"No, ma'am. Not me."

"Looks like you'd have stayed away from the outlaw business, if being in jail bothers you so much."

"Yeah, looks like it."

"So how come?"

"Why do people do anything?"

"Like the mountain. You climbed it because it

was there?"

"Something like that."

"That's a bunch of crap," she said. "Don't give me that."

"What's it to you, anyway?"

"Maybe a lot. I want to know."

"Look. I did something I shouldn't have and got thrown into prison. I was trying to correct a mistake society made, and it turns out society didn't want to be corrected. I should have known that. Then I get out, finally, in one piece, with a little sanity left, and they've thrown me out of my profession. People I knew turned the other way when they saw me. Nobody wanted me working for them. A man's got to do something with himself. I drank. I partied. I got into my old Vietnam frame of mind. I was the tough guy, the one who's smarter than the rest, the one who can't be whipped. I got that swagger back in my step.

"I was disgusting when I was in Vietnam, and I knew it even back then. But I guess I felt I had to be that way to survive. As long as I was tough, hard, and mean, I was okay. Anytime I softened up, bad things happened, friends got killed because I did the wrong thing. A Vietnamese girl killed herself because of something I did, or maybe something I didn't do. Can you imagine being in a war zone and committing suicide, for Christ's sake? So I got tough, and stayed tough.

"When I got out of prison, it was the same way.

A war. My damn wife had left me and remarried. People hated my guts, just because I'd tried to have a little integrity and do the right thing. And on top of all that, I'd gotten caught while I was doing it. I'd failed, I'd flopped, I'd blown it. I found some new people, people who didn't know so much about me. It was easy. The bars and juke joints are full of people. Drive a fancy car, buy enough drinks, tip waitresses with a ten-dollar bill stuffed down a brassiere, and you make friends. But these folks were different. Instead of ripping off the world from behind a desk somewhere, figuring the tax angles and overhead and how to swap good material for cheap stuff, these people did it all head-on. They said, okay, we're going to break the law, because that's how we live, that's what we are. Now, try and catch us.

"There was something appealing about that. It sounds funny, but there was a crazy kind of honesty to it. They seemed like better people than the ones I grew up with. The money looked good, too. It was something I fell into. I played the tough guy. I did some drugs and some wild stuff, like everybody else. Then somebody made me an offer to run some up from Colombia, knowing I had airplanes and liked to fly. It was an easy thing to get into."

"But harder to get out of," she said.

"You know it."

"It was a game with you, then."

"Not exactly. More a contest of will."

"I don't know what that means."

"Neither do I."

"So it was a game, and now this is an even bigger one."

"This is the ultimate game."

"You want to beat them. What do you call them? The Cocaine Cowboys. You want to beat them because they're such bad guys. Or what?"

"I guess. I never liked them. They kill people for no reason at all, just to see the blood flow. They get their kicks from things that made me sick, and, like I told you, I try to be Mister Tough Guy. Human life means nothing to these people. Nothing is sacred. They have no god, no dreams, no hopes, nothing but this moment they're living. They don't care about the lives they ruin thousands of miles away, people who crash and burn-out that they'll never see or have to deal with. They never think even once about people gone crazy, or mothers crying over graves, or children wondering what happened to daddy."

"You, either," she said. "You never think about those things. You said everybody has a choice, and it's not your place to make the choice for people. Something like that."

"You're right. I tried to forget all that. Tried to ignore it. By that time, my own choice was gone. See, once you're in with these people, once you're a Cocaine Cowboy yourself, the only way out is to die. I wasn't ready to quit, not that ready."

"And now you are. You want the Cowboys to pay."

"That's right."

"You want to get your own way. Again."

"Always."

"It seems to me that if you're really concerned about the children and mothers and the crazy folks, you can't just sell this stuff to somebody who's going to put it out on the streets," she said. "I mean, that's if you really care."

"I guess. I don't know. If they don't get it here, they'll get it somewhere else. I don't see why you're worried about it. You're the one who used to wear the little silver spoon on a chain around your neck."

"I don't any more," she said. "The funny thing is, it always scared me. Every time, I thought something bad would happen. Even back at the club with the other dancers a long time ago, we'd do a little that somebody would give us to get close to us, and that would scare me. I got to the point it scared me so much that I acted like it didn't mean a thing. I'd still do it if somebody was watching. It's that peer pressure thing, I guess. But not by myself. Then Wilson came along, and if you weren't into coke already, he'd make it his business to get you on it. That was his main thing in life, other than women. The coke and the women kind of went together. I had to act like it was a big deal. That was what he wanted. That was my way of protecting myself. If you were stuffing it up your nose all the time, you were cool. If you weren't, you weren't cool. I didn't want to do it all the time, so I made it seem like I was."

"So you talked about it more than you did it. It was mostly an act."

"Yeah."

"That's weird."

"Okay, I'm a little weird. I admit it."

"A little?"

"That was my defense."

"So you never liked it."

"Not really. Maybe a little."

"And every time I made a run to Colombia and back, it cut another chunk out of my soul."

"We're a pair, huh?"

"I think we're both nuts."

"Could be."

"I think people should have the guts to just do what they want to do, not what they think they have to do. If you could say, no, you're not going to touch that stuff because it scares you, you ought to do it. If you want to quit, you ought to quit. Instead, we sit around and try to impress each other and wonder what'll happen if we quit. If. If is the problem."

They started climbing again. Hutto felt lighter now, as they neared the top. He scrambled a little faster, and she kept up, grunting all the way. He looked back occasionally at the view, watching the birds soaring on the air currents. He remembered

Elizabeth's desire to fly. Everybody wants to do what they can't. Everybody wants the impossible.

That's why we have hang gliders, Hutto thought. He loved his airplanes, but wouldn't strap himself into a hang glider for all the coca plants in South America. That's too much like a bird.

He was thinking about this when he reached the top. He saw three men standing there wearing daypacks. Not tourists, he thought. Something was wrong. One was wearing shiny street shoes, loafers with tassles, another had on new Nike running shoes. The third wore hiking boots.

The one with the hiking boots, taller and broader than Hutto, with dark hair and a neat mustache, smiled when he saw him come over the edge. Hutto put a hand near the pocket of the backpack holding one of his pistols. The man kept smiling.

"Help the lady up," he said when Elizabeth crawled to the top.

Hutto reached back and pulled her to his side. Now he could see that the man held a shiny German-made revolver in his right hand, slipped from a hidden pocket when Hutto turned.

"Glad to see you again, Hutto," he said. "My people are very, very disappointed in you."

"I can imagine."

"Aren't you going to introduce me?" the man said.

"Elizabeth, this is Chico," he said. "Chico kills people for a living."

"It's my pleasure," Chico said to her, and smiled the smile that worked charms in nightclubs across the world.

## Chapter Thirteen

Chico stood tapping the pistol barrel against the palm of his left hand. He kept smiling, looking openly at Elizabeth. His teeth were big and white. Caps, probably, Hutto thought.

"Just hiking, or looking for something here?" he asked.

"There's nothing here," Hutto said.

"Nothing at all?"

"It's gone."

"I suppose the little birds and bees and bears have gobbled it up."

"Something like that."

"So there's no point in retracing your steps?"

"No."

Still beating time with the pistol, Chico turned to his two soldiers. "Ramon, Luis, search him. The girl, too. Be careful. The girl is the dangerous one, as always."

"Woman," Elizabeth said.

"No difference," Chico answered.

Ramon and Luis were more thorough than Axel

158

had been. They found both pistols, all the ammunition clips, and both knives. Hutto stood calmly through the shakedown. Elizabeth squirmed a bit under the Colombians' touch.

"You're the Cowboys," she said.

"What cowboys?" Chico asked.

"The Cocaine Cowboys. Hutto talked about you."

"We were expected, then."

"Anticipated," Hutto said.

"Cowboys. John Wayne, Jesse James, Wyatt Earp," Chico said. "Which one are we?"

"It's your gun. You be whoever you want," Hutto said.

"Funny man. You're always a funny man."

"You two know each other?" Elizabeth asked.

"We have met. Business necessities, and such," Chico said.

"Chico hangs around Baranquilla and snarls whenever the big boys want to trot out their pet lion."

"My bite is worse than my snarl, friend."

"He's their big bouncer. Only instead of throwing you out of the bar or out of town, he throws you off the edge of the world. He's supposed to be able to kill you a hundred different ways—from bare hands to bombs—and leave no evidence, no untidy remains."

"A hundred ways, it's all the same," Chico said.

"So why don't you shoot?" Elizabeth asked.

"Oh, my lady, we can't be so discourteous, so abrupt. We have so many things to discuss. You understand, of course, if I desire your company and Hutto's wit and conversation."

"You've sure got a big mouth on you," she said.

"We should be civil in all things. This includes you, pretty lady."

"How'd you find us?" she asked.

"You two should really be more discreet. People see things, hear things. With a little help, they remember. Gatlinburg is, after all, a rather small town. I'm good at helping people remember. Plus, that Jeep is rather obvious, don't you think? One more thing, we had our own tracking device in this load, and it came down here. We must be prepared in case of plane crashes or other unfortunate accidents. All we had to do was wait."

Chico pulled his own Klecko from a pocket, tossed it in the air, and smiled that big smile. "It's fate, I would say," he said.

He put the pistol in his daypack and stood looking over the edge at the clouds accumulating in the valleys below. "So beautiful," he said. "Of course, entirely different from the Andes or the Alps or even your own Rockies. But lovely, nonetheless."

"I never thought of you as the outdoors type," Hutto said.

"You might be surprised by many things about me."

"I guess you're just a well-rounded personality."

"A man in my position has time and money to learn and enjoy many things, if he only will."

"I heard you were some kind of nut about

Shakespeare."

"You did? Going home, I hope to travel to Montgomery, Alabama, to the magnificent theater there to see their production of *King Lear*. An unforgettable theater. Superior to anything in New York or London."

"Of course, you're a poet, too. All hit men are poets, right?"

"Don't get too funny, Hutto. My poetry is sadly deficient. But I appreciate the masters. The Irishman, William Butler Yeats, wrote something somehow appropriate here. It came to mind as we hiked. 'Too long a sacrifice makes a stone of the heart,' he wrote. It's from his great poem, *Easter 1916*, about his countrymen's attempt to overthrow British rule by overtaking the post office building in Dublin. After a week they were all killed or captured. The British executed the leaders. MacDonagh, MacBride, Connolly, and Pearse, I believe they were. 'Too long a sacrifice makes a stone of the heart.' I like that sentiment."

"You know a lot about it," Elizabeth said.

"A lot for a Spic, you say? A lot for a Cocaine Cowboy? Perhaps I am different from what you expected. Maybe I am struggling against that heart of stone. Like you, perhaps."

"Perhaps," she said.

"Why all the intellectual babble, Chico?" Hutto asked.

"It's my way. You should know that."

"Just shoot us and get it over with."

"Such a hurry," Chico said. "No, I want to understand you first."

"That'll make it easier for you?"

"No. Infinitely harder. That's the way I want it. That's the only way."

"Look, Chico, we're all real impressed with your sensitivity, but I don't understand what you're trying to do," Hutto said.

"What's to understand?"

"You wanted to understand us. Why can't we understand you?"

"A difficult task," he said. "Come on. Let's return to the source of all our difficulties."

"What?" Elizabeth said.

"He wants us to take him to the stuff," Hutto said.

"Don't you already know where it is?" she asked.

"It's so much easier if you just show us," Chico said.

He directed Ramon and Luis ahead on the trail and put himself in the rear with the prisoners between them.

"Why did you do it? You always seemed like a smart man. An attorney. Educated," Chico said.

"That's why," Hutto answered.

"It wasn't smart."

"Looked smart to me."

"And with Wilson, too. Wilson was such a fool."

"He could get the job done."

"Not this time."

"No, this time he blew it."

"This time was doomed from the start. Did you presume to think you could cross my people and survive? Or did you have a death wish?"

"We could have gotten away with it, if everything went right."

"And the girl? Why sacrifice her for your foolish plan?"

"She was just here. I couldn't do it without her, and she was already involved. So I took her with me."

"I see. Couldn't do it without her, and couldn't do it with her. Obviously. And, of course, the Italians are your buyers for this shipment."

"Of course."

"Only they would have the money and the stupidity to attempt it."

"You could look at it that way," Hutto said.

"It's hard to understand. The real Italians, the ones in Italy, are such an interesting people. Artistic, with a certain genius for architecture and the fable, though certainly not for government. In all, a fascinating nation. And the Italian-Americans, as well, merging that background with the new world. But these Italian mobsters, these crooks, are ruined, thwarted, backward people. Beasts of a modern sort. And you deal with them."

"It's the business they're in."

"It has made a stone of their hearts."

"Right."

"Did you really suppose you could hide from us?" Chico asked.

"Yes, I did. I think the world is big enough so that even the Cowboys can't cover it all."

"Foolish. If you were on the moon, and we really wanted you, we could get you. I followed a man into Antarctica one time. He had a terrible accident on an island of ice. We are *so* good at finding our man, that sometimes I think perhaps even *I* could not hide from us, if I wanted to. The only way to hide is in the grave. And who wants to hide there?"

"I think you have an overblown confidence in your abilities, Chico."

"Not at all. I am good. They say each person has a skill, a secret of sorts, that is theirs alone. This, I am sorry to say, is mine. I'm better at this than anyone alive. Not even the Israelis can come close to me."

"You'll make a mistake sometime," Hutto said. "Some hotshot kid with a plastic bomb in a briefcase will put you away."

"No, Hutto, I think not. I'll retire before I grow that careless."

"You're careless now."

"And how is that."

"We're alive, aren't we? If that's not careless, I don't know what is."

"But you serve a purpose by being alive."

"What purpose is that?"

"Mine. Mine alone."

"Not the Cowboys'?"

"Sometimes my purpose and the Cowboys' purpose are not the same."

"What's that supposed to mean."

"Just keep walking, my friend. Walk down this mountain, and think how good God must have felt when he created this, and looked down at it and saw its beauty before man ever set foot here soiling it."

"If you ever do retire, you can always get a job here as a park ranger," Hutto said.

"That is a pleasant thought."

"You could lecture tourists about the habits of the black bear, and in your spare time you could sit up here and read Yeats."

"Don't forget Shakespeare."

"Yeah, him, too."

"Perhaps they'd not hire Colombians, though."

"Maybe not. You'd have to quit saying perhaps so much, too."

"A habit. Some Americans say you know. I say perhaps."

They dropped below the 6,000-foot level and the spruce and fir gave way to the more familiar oaks and birches and hemlocks. Hutto spotted some trillium huddling alone under the large trees. Some hikers were down the trail, waiting for a woman who was off urinating in the bushes.

"What if we run up to them and say, 'Help, help, the Cocaine Cowboys have got us'?" Elizabeth said.

"I hope you will not do that. I hate to kill the innocent. And, even if you succeeded, after sitting in prison a few years—which is where you would surely go—perhaps you would wish Ramon and

Luis and I had finished you off here. It's not so much fun in prison."

"You would know about prison, I guess."

"As a young man, I spent time in a particularly disgusting one in my country."

"What for?"

"Killing a man. What else?"

"How'd you get out?" she wanted to know.

"The Cowboys, as you call them, helped me escape. I met some of their minor members in prison. They decided I would be useful to them. They gave me a new life. This one."

"I was in prison, too," Hutto said.

"Yes, I know. For killing a man, also?"

"No, nothing like that. A minor thing, really. But a man did get killed. The man I tried to save."

"A terrible thing. You'll have to tell me about it."

"Too long a story, and there's nothing to tell, anyway. Now, your life, Chico. That's a story. You ought to write a book."

"And give away my secrets? Perhaps posthumously."

They passed the group of hikers, three men and three women, all in shorts with hiking boots and thick socks. "How far to the top?" they asked.

"Not far to Mount Kephart," Chico said. "Much farther to Le Conte."

"Thanks," they said, and moved on. Hutto heard the men talking about football as they moved up the trail.

"You've done your homework," Hutto said.

"Always."

"Why so thorough?"

"It keeps me alive."

"Would you kill a woman?" Elizabeth asked.

"Only if necessary. Just like a man."

"Well, I vote we give you the stuff. You take it, and we'll go on our way. No problems. Forget and forgive or something like that," she said.

"But it doesn't work that way," Chico said. "You commit a crime against my people, and we have to respond. If we don't, others will follow you. Then where would we be? I will certainly dislike killing one as lovely as you, but surely you must see my position. I could not return to Colombia and say, 'I liked her, so I let the woman live,' or, 'They were sorry, so I took the cocaine back and let them go.' You can understand this, can't you?"

"Oh, sure, you're not the one getting your head blown off," she said.

"Perhaps we can think of something more acceptable than that."

"And you're the one talking about turning hearts to stone. You can't even have a heart. All that smooth talking, then, boom, just kill us. I can't even believe there are people like you walking around, talking about Shakespeare and Yeats, whoever he is, and killing people with the same breath," she said.

"It is not quite that way. I do only what I must."

"Right. Bastard," she said.

"It has nothing to do with personal feelings. I

may like you and value you highly, but I have no choice in the ultimate."

"How many people have you killed?" she asked.

"I don't keep count."

"Come on. You must know how many."

"I'm not Billy the Kid, with notches on my pistol."

"Okay, then, let's guess. Five? Ten?"

"Ten times ten at the minimum."

"A hundred people," she said. "Minimum."

"Yes. I am not ashamed of it. Many deserved to die. Hardly any were so charming as you, Elizabeth."

"Go to hell," she said.

"Not yet. It looks as though you will precede me."

"You," she said, "just go to hell and leave me alone."

"Would that I could."

"It's his job," Hutto said.

"Yes. Listen to your man," Chico said.

"He's not my man."

"Chico is a workman, a technician," Hutto said.

"That's correct," Chico said.

"Like hell."

"Maybe we should be friendly. Maybe it might work out better in the end, if we cooperate," Hutto said.

"I think you are beginning to understand," Chico said. "I think you see there is a way for us all to keep our dignity."

"I'd rather keep breathing," she said.

"Let's not turn our hearts to stone," Chico said. "The last line of that poem reads, 'A terrible beauty is born.' Perhaps we can make that, the three of us."

"You're weird," Elizabeth said.

"But I am alive, and I plan to stay that way for a long, long time."

"Me, too," she said.

Chico laughed, a long roll deep within his chest, and even Elizabeth smiled. Hutto watched them and wondered about it all. Chico was just another example of a world gone crazy.

## Chapter Fourteen

They came down the mountain, a little troop tossed from heaven. Leaving the Appalachian Canada behind, they passed through birch and beech at 5,000 feet, with rhododendron, laurel, and azalea, and the old places of the chestnut forest (which long ago fell to a quick and deadly disease), and came to the region of the tulip poplar, huge and straight, flinging themselves skyward. Here there was oak and hickory, dogwood and locust, ash and basswood, and trees Hutto knew but could not name.

He wished Chico would pronounce their sentence. If he had just walked up and shot them, Hutto could have understood it better. From the Cowboys' awed boasts, Hutto knew Chico ordinarily wasted no time. He did the job fast, neatly, and was back in Colombia or maybe Finland or New Zealand, even Japan, before the cops discovered one of their citizens had stopped breathing.

Now Chico jacked them around, quoting poetry, chatting about Shakespeare, teasing them with talk about everyone keeping their dignity. Hutto couldn't figure it. First, Riley let them beat him because he had to impress them with his conquests. Then Chico comes along, acting like an intellectual, talking about trying to understand them before he did whatever it was he was planning to do.

He who hesitates gets stomped, Hutto reasoned. That's how it was in Vietnam. That's how it is now, though most people don't realize it. That's why they get stomped.

Chico walked behind him, the big boots with soles like off-road tires crunching into the trail. His stride was smooth and long. He was bigger, faster, stronger, and in better shape than Hutto, and he had not spent three days thrashing around the mountains carrying eighty or ninety pounds on his back. He had not beaten off cannibals the previous night. He appeared to be one of those guys who do a thousand sit-ups every morning, then go out for a nice ten-mile run.

His partners were something else entirely, and Hutto wondered just how they'd been picked for this mission. Ramon looked scared and uneasy, tripping along in his new Nike running shoes. He wore old battered jeans and a new red flannel shirt. He led the column and kept looking back at them to make sure everyone was still following.

Luis was crippling himself in his shiny street shoes. The tassels were flopping around with each step, and Hutto could tell he was getting blisters, big ones. They'd be watery sores of pus tomorrow, and he'd have trouble walking. He wore tan gabardine pants—the kind the stores call sports slacks—and a bright green shirt with an alligator sewed onto the left side of the chest.

Both Ramon and Luis wore daypacks. Hutto knew they were full of weapons, including his own. He guessed Ramon was in training, since he was younger, trying to pick up tips on the art of murder from the old master. Luis would be along to keep the other two straight, to prevent them from going bad. Hutto thought he might be trouble. He had a rummy look about him, and tough, tight little eyes that held no compassion for anyone.

They came to a big rock by the trail and sat on it for a rest. A chipmunk peeked out at them as they drank water. Hutto nodded at Luis and said, "Couldn't you have gotten this one a better pair of shoes?"

Chico laughed. "Luis does not want to appear to be a poor dresser. He has too much stubborn pride. For Luis, impressing is more important than comfort."

"He's going to regret it in the morning."

"Yes. Perhaps he will have to be put out of his misery, like a horse gone lame."

Luis spoke for the first time. "I take care of myself," he told Hutto. "I am a gentleman, a businessman."

"A gentleman from the slums of Baranquilla," Chico said.

"Like you. A man's birth does not make him

what he is," Luis said.

"True," Chico said. "But a man whose life is spent running from his birth is a lonely man.".

Luis turned away and flicked a rock at the chipmunk, which vanished.

"Ramon has more sense," Hutto said.

"About shoes, perhaps. He comes from a wealthy family who met with misfortune. Now he is determined to avenge his father by taking money from the very ones who destroyed him. Ramon is an unusual fellow."

"Speak English?"

"Very well, but only when he must, such as around the young ladies."

Ramon said something in Spanish. Chico answered in a quick gutteral burst. Hutto, who knew some Spanish, couldn't pick up what they said, but he suspected Ramon objected to Chico's description and told him so.

If Ramon was training to be a killer, he had probably picked the right profession. His eyes were hard and set deep in his young face. If he could get rid of that uncertainty about himself, he'd be able to pull a trigger on anybody. From a double-crossing delivery man, to a good-looking hooker who knew too much, to a baby with a face right off the picture on the diaper box, and for no other reason but to make the parents understand he meant business. But for now, Ramon looked for Chico to lead. He wouldn't pull his gun until Chico had already blown away the target. He'd be slow, worried, unsure. Now, he could be taken. In a couple of years, he'd be a rock, without emotion. It would take someone like Chico to get him then.

"I thought you usually worked alone," Hutto said.

"I prefer to," Chico said. "But my people decided that you were such a big fish, they better send out a boatload of fishermen. Perhaps they were afraid bad things would happen to a man acting alone."

"Perhaps they're right."

"Yes, sometimes they know best."

"And sometimes they don't."

"Well, it only takes one hook to catch the fish. If you use the right bait."

"What bait's that?" Hutto asked.

Chico just fingered his mustache, turning the corners down at the edge of his mouth. Hutto looked at him, wondering if Chico was running a scam of his own. He didn't think he could take much suspense. It had been a long, hard day, and not a particularly good one.

Elizabeth looked tired. The descent and climb at the Jumpoff had worn her down. First she'd had the disappointment of not getting the stuff after they'd crawled down the mountain. Then, running into Chico and the Cowboys had shocked her. If their encounter with Riley and Axel and the boys had been terrifying, hiking with Chico as he chattered about E.E. Cummings and Tennessee Williams, T.S. Elliott and Yeats, Yeats, and more Yeats, with, naturally, a little Shakespeare thrown in, was too much. It was like being a condemned prisoner walking to the electric chair with an executioner who talked about what he was going to do tomorrow, going to the lake with his kids, maybe playing a little roundball.

Chico was too calculating, too cool. What he meant by all this, what he said silently was, *Hey, gotta kill you, no hard feelings, okay? Nice try and all that, but you blew it, and now I have to do my thing. So let's be friends all the while, okay?*

Hutto didn't get it. He'd never killed professionally, at least not getting paid specifically to do it, so he didn't know how hit men worked. But if it had been him, he wouldn't let himself get too close to the victims. He'd ignore them, maybe act like they were dirt under his feet. But he wouldn't buddy up to them.

Maybe talking like an intellectual was Chico's way of distancing himself from all this. What's a little Strindberg- or Chekov-talk matter on the way to the big blowout? Let's put our minds on the higher things, on the level of the gods, while our bodies grub it out in the mud.

Hutto wished Chico would kill them here, dump their bodies in a washout under a big rock somewhere. The wild pigs might get them, but Hutto preferred being up in the clean air where the stars still twinkled at night, to spending eternity in a hole somewhere down in the flatlands. He wanted to push the issue now, turn and try to whip Chico on the trail, then take on Ramon and Luis.

He'd never get more than one step on Chico. And if he did, Ramon might be fast and sure with Chico gone. He couldn't make that move, so he kept walking, listening to Chico's steps behind. Besides, it was possible, not likely, but remotely possible, that Elizabeth might make it out of this alive if Hutto worked it right. She might have to do some things she wouldn't like, but if it saved her neck, she couldn't argue.

Somehow he couldn't see Elizabeth dead, that big sleek body gone slack. It was all up to Chico. It was his play, and, so far, he seemed to be having a great time walking around the mountains talking about literature with a capital *L*. It didn't matter to him at all that Hutto, at least at this moment, had absolutely no interest in such things, or that Elizabeth hadn't even graduated from high school, much less read Shakespeare. That might work in Elizabeth's favor, Hutto thought. Chico might see her as a reclamation project, a *My Fair Lady* of the hills.

Then Hutto tripped over a root in the trail, and that pushed those ridiculous daydreams from his mind. Chico had come here to kill them both, and he'd do it. Hutto knew that.

Chico finally seemed to have decided they'd had enough talk about books and plays and poetry. He was silent awhile, then said, "You are thinking perhaps of death?"

"Wouldn't you?" Hutto said.

"I think of it every day. It is with me always."

"Naturally," Elizabeth said.

"If I were you, I would contemplate the meaning of death and life everlasting."

"I know about death," Elizabeth said. "It means you've crapped out. Permanently."

"And the life after?"

"You believe in that?" she said.

"Most certainly."

"How can you go around killing people for a living, if you believe in heaven and hell?" Hutto asked.

"How can you go around selling dangerous drugs to children?" Chico asked him.

"You're doing that, too."

"No. No drugs."

"But you're working for them."

"The servant can work for his master and not be a part of that master's business."

"Not with the Cowboys."

"Yes. Even with the Cowboys."

"But if you believe in heaven and hell, you're deliberately dooming yourself."

"Your opinion."

"What about 'Thou shalt not kill'?"

"I have to live with myself on that. Perhaps it is different from your impression. Perhaps I am actually doing God's will, in my own way."

"Perhaps you're crazy."

"Who can say?"

They walked down, down, down the trail to Newfound Gap, passing several groups of young people joking with each other, and some couples meandering along. The parking lot was full. Ramon went to the restroom. Luis sat down on the stone wall and pulled off his shoes. His dark silk socks were sticky with blood. Chico talked to him in Spanish. Hutto thought he called Luis a fool, but wasn't sure.

"If I want to see this many people, I can go to New York City or Rio," Chico said.

"They say sixty thousand people a day come to the park in summer," Hutto told him. "Most never make it off the main roads. They go to Gatlinburg, then take a quick run out to about here, and turn around and go back to town. They spend most of their time buying ceramic frogs and Christmas tree ornaments and eating pancakes and greaseburgers."

"I have little need for ceramic frogs."

"How about pink and green flashing Jesuses?"

"Not for them, either."

"Of course, you can go the other way, down to Cherokee, North Carolina, and buy made-in-Korea moccasins from the remnants of the brave and noble Indians who refused to move to Oklahoma and withstood all the pressure the U.S. government could put on them, only to have the freedom to produce descendants who could stand along the roadside in ridiculous war bonnets—which the Cherokees never wore in the first place—charging tourists five bucks a picture to pose with children and stand by worn-out bears in chicken wire cages."

"You sound disgusted."

"I am."

"Disgust is a good thing. It can lead to change."

"For those who live long enough."

"Correct."

"I don't suppose we can work anything out?" Hutto said.

"Don't suppose anything at this time."

"Quit teasing us," Elizabeth said.

"Teasing? I am not teasing."

"This is like torturing a wounded animal."

"I'm neither teasing nor torturing. I'm merely doing my business and trying to conduct myself civilly."

"With dignity," Hutto said.

"Bull," Elizabeth said.

Chico rose to his full height and looked down at Hutto. His eyes came alive, flashing bright.

"Don't push it," he said.

He walked to the edge, looking at row upon row of ridges stretching far into North Carolina. "It's lovely out there," he said. "Then just turn around and see these cars and these people and it's two worlds, not even close. These mountains have a character unlike anything else. But people are the same everywhere, more or less."

"These mountains are older than the Alps," Hutto said. "When India bumped into Asia and created the Himalayas, these mountains were already old. The Rockies have no history at all compared to the Smokies. The rocks here are so old that they're mostly granite. They're so ancient they don't even have fossils. They've been worn down, grain by grain, these hills have. They're old, but they're still wild. They're like an old man sitting around a shopping mall somewhere swapping stores with his buddies. There are people everywhere, but he doesn't see them. He's still the cockiest old coot in town. That's what these mountains are. Friendly sometimes, but still the cockiest thing around."

"You know them well," Chico said.

"As well as they've let me."

## Chapter Fifteen

Ramon came up the asphalt walkway from the restroom and stopped to watch a black-haired girl, about twenty years old, bounce by. Hutto saw her, too, and even Chico watched her prance along, swaying from side to side, wearing tight white shorts and a top that barely contained her. She had pale skin, the kind that shows its veins in a faint blue map of life. Probably a local girl, Hutto figured. Local, riding around with a boyfriend, drinking a twelve-pack of beer.

She went across the parking lot, with them watching her every step, to a car that looked familiar. Hutto had seen those scratches before, had studied this car, and then nearly forgotten it. But this was it, unmistakably. Riley's car.

Riley's car. And then, when she sat down in the battered front seat, Hutto looked at Riley come back to life. Riley resurrected. Riley a la Lazarus. A man sat there with Riley's hair and Riley's beard. Even sitting behind the steering wheel he looked big, lanky, and strong. He had that look on his face that said he cared for nothing in the world, not even this bouncing beauty settling in beside him, stroking his shoulder across the seat back.

Elizabeth saw him, too. "Oh, my God," she said, and propped herself against the stone wall at the edge of the drop-off.

Chico looked at her, then back to Hutto. "You know this girl?" he asked.

"No. The man with her looks familiar."

"Say hello, then, if you wish."

"I don't think so. He's supposed to be dead."

"How do you know this?"

"We're the ones that killed him, or we thought we did."

"This was when?"

"A million years ago. Last night, I guess."

"You are sure? Perhaps your shots missed."

"No. We shot him three times point-blank, once between the eyes, then blew up a bomb on his stomach, and buried him under ten thousand tons of rock."

"Then I say this is not your man."

"Looks just like him."

"Impossible. Every man I ever dynamited stayed dynamited."

"It's his car."

"Don't worry about it. You killed him once. You can kill him again, if necessary."

"I can't believe this," Elizabeth said. "He just won't die. I told you. I told you up in the cave he wouldn't die. Now he's back."

182

"Hold on," Hutto said.

"One time I killed a man in Montreal," Chico said. "It was impossible that he could live. Then in Atlanta two months later, I saw him again. He had the same appearance exactly. So, I killed him again, and it turned out he was a different man entirely. Innocent of the charges I brought against him, though undoubtedly guilty of something. But for my purposes, innocent. His crime was looking like someone else. There are certain facial types that repeat through our race. These people all look similar, perhaps even like twins. This could be that."

"You've got an answer for everything, don't you?" Elizabeth said.

"Not everything. But I am not one to believe in backwoods voodoo. Either a man is dead, or he's alive. There's nothing in the middle."

"Come to the Great Smoky Mountains, land of the walking dead," Ramon said.

It was the first English sentence Hutto had heard him say. Chico turned to him and started to say something, then didn't.

"It walks, it talks, it takes a dump just like a real human," Hutto said.

"I were you, I be quiet," Ramon said.

"Don't start," Chico said. So they stopped glaring at each other and looked again at the old Buick. The girl leaned over to the man and tongued his ear. He pulled her close and reached a big hand down the top of her shirt and slowly massaged a large, soft breast. Then he pushed away, toward the passenger side door, and concentrated on something across the way, in the direction of Hutto and Chico and their nervous little group.

"Shall we go?" Chico finally said.

"Might as well," Hutto said.

"If you'd like, we can kill this man, then go about our business."

"No. We've already killed him once, and I don't know the girl."

"Perhaps I can do a better job than you."

"With your vast experience, I'm sure you could. Like you said, though, it could be a coincidence, a mistake."

"Yes. Yours."

"It's probably just one of those look-alike deals."

"Let a man go who deserves to die, and perhaps you are the one who winds up dead."

"Looks like we're going to wind up that way anyhow, so what difference does it make?"

"As you wish," Chico said.

He directed Hutto and Elizabeth to the car he and the other two had arrived in, and put Ramon and Luis in the Jeep. He told Elizabeth to drive, and sat in the back seat.

"There is more cocaine to be found, right?" he said.

"One more batch," Hutto said.

"How much is that?"

"A hundred and forty pounds."

"You are ambitious."

"So damn ambitious he's getting me killed," Elizabeth said.

"Drive to this batch, as you call it. Then we'll see who gets killed," Chico said.

She put her hand on the key and gave Hutto a confused look. When he just shook his head, she started the car and made a left turn out of the parking lot. The Riley look-alike stared at them all the way. His black-haired beauty seemed preoccupied with some children playing on the asphalt in the other direction. Ramon drove the Jeep following them, with Luis slumped in the seat beside him, rubbing his wounded feet.

Hutto told her to turn right at the Clingmans Dome road. Chico insisted she slow down so they wouldn't attract the attention of any enforcement rangers.

"I need my Klecko," Hutto said.

"And I need my mother," Chico said.

"No, really. If we're going to find this stuff, I have to have my Klecko. Yours won't work. It must be on a different frequency than mine, or I'd have picked it up when I found that last bundle."

So Chico had Elizabeth pull over and told Ramon to look in the backpacks and find the tracking device. He brought it to the car, tossing it up and down like a baseball.

"Careful, fool," Hutto said.

"We'll see who's a fool," Ramon said, and handed it to him.

Elizabeth drove on. Chico sat silent in the back and Hutto concentrated on the Klecko device. The reading got a little stronger when they passed Mount Collins, rising nearly 6,200 feet to their right. Hutto remembered pushing the pack of coke out a little after the plane passed Clingmans Dome. Nearly as many people walked the half mile to the tower there as parked and stared into the distance at Newfound Gap. He'd been afraid he'd hit the parking area or near a heavily traveled trail. It had been dark, so it was hard to tell just what he'd been doing, but he knew they should be coming to it soon.

That had been eons ago, that night when he had crouched in the back of the Cessna and deposited gift-wrapped packages all over the Smokies. Eons and several dead men ago.

Too many dead men. He hoped he could avoid being one of them.

He looked back at Chico, who smiled at him, one of those fake Cocaine Cowboy grins he probably put on just before ripping your heart out. "Okay, Chico, it's you and me," Hutto said. "Forget your buddies back there and forget her. Neither of us wants to die, but somebody is going to. So let's deal."

"No deals," Chico said.

"Dealing is your only way out."

"*My* only way?"

"That's right. You'll never get out of this alive."

"Let me see," Chico said. "It seems to me I have the weapons. I have the army. You have nothing but yourself."

"That's all I need."

"You're a foolish man. Only a fool would even attempt to cross my people. Only a fool would try to deal with me. But you have courage. It's too bad foolishness blinds you."

"Okay, then, just kill me right here and get it over with."

"We must recover this batch first."

"Why? We already lost what the bear ate and the one that exploded back there where you found us."

"My orders are to recover the cocaine and kill you. I'll carry them out."

"I don't have to take you to it."

"I don't have to be nice when I kill you, either."

"I'm shaking," Hutto said.

"You can die easy or you can die hard. It's so much better when the victim cooperates. There's less pain and heartache. The body is easier to identify. It's a shame when my assignments don't cooperate."

"One more chance, Chico. You can take my offer and retire anywhere in the world you want. You can buy all the girls you need or original Shakespeare folios. You name it."

"You insult me. When I take an assignment, I fulfill it."

"Okay," Hutto said. "You don't have to whine about it. That was your last chance. Now I'll have no recourse but to whip your ass."

"You're pushing."

"Damn right. I push hard."

"I have only so much patience," Chico said. "I'm a gentle man, until I'm pushed."

"Who cares what you are?"

They rode in silence along the spine of the mountain for awhile. "Tell me, why did you try this?" Chico asked.

"Money and the peace it buys."

"There's no peace in money."

"Maybe I did it so I could see if I could beat you."

"Beating me is out of the question."

"No, it isn't."

"How much would you have gotten?"

"We were shooting for $300 million. Now we've lost two packs, plus Wilson's. So, I don't know exactly. Maybe a total of $180 or $200 million. Somewhere in that range."

"You say a bear ate one."

"Yes."

"Several million dollars American down a bear's gut."

"Pretty sickening, huh?"

"Even more for the bear, I bet."

"It killed him."

"Many creatures will die for this cocaine before the end of this."

Hutto had been watching the readings on the Klecko get stronger, the beeping light more insistent. When they came to the little parking area at the Noland Divide trail, a mile and a half from the top, he told Elizabeth to stop.

"We're here," he said.

With the pistol, Chico motioned them from the car. Ramon got out of the Jeep and wanted to know what was going on. Chico jabbered at him in Spanish, and he went back to the Jeep and told Luis. Hutto saw them gesturing, heard the speech without understanding a word. Luis didn't like the idea, he could see that. Luis would fight them all the way about this hike. They had caught their prey, now they should dispose of it, go home, and soak their aching feet, was probably what he was saying.

So Chico left Luis there, watching things from the Jeep. Chico put a pack on Ramon, another on Hutto, and wore a daypack himself. Hutto heard the weapons clanking within it.

He read the Klecko and didn't listen to Elizabeth's complaints. They went a couple of miles, mostly in grunting silence, to a place called Roundtop Knob, a bald with laurel spreading across it. All the way there, except for Elizabeth's grousing, no one talked. The hat was soft, the stones few, and the roots out of the way. They moved quickly.

At the knob, Hutto dropped down the side toward Clingmans Creek, struggling a little through the undergrowth, hurrying to find the pack before dark. He didn't understand just why he was working so hard. Maybe he just wanted to get this little adventure over, one way or the other. The pack was down about a quarter of a mile from the knob, still in good shape. Some bushes caught the chute. Ramon cut it loose and buried it while they checked the stuff. Good as new.

Hutto and Ramon divided it among themselves, except about twenty pounds which they put in Elizabeth's daypack, the one Luis had carried earlier. Climbing back to the top with sixty pounds was hard, but Hutto was used to it by now. Ramon complained the whole way, slipping, fighting the weight. Hutto could tell Ramon had never done much hiking and camping. He'd probably never been in a real army.

They made the top, and with little talk Chico pointed the way. They set off up the trail as the sun faded behind Clingmans Dome. Chico was in a hurry now, eager to accomplish his mission, pushing them hard through oak and beech trees. Ramon's struggles with the pack irritated Chico, so he made him go first, nearly jogging with it, a kind of backwoods torture for the Colombian dandy. Hutto thought Chico was contemplating killing Ramon, too. Eliminating the competition.

He never got a chance to know for sure.

They came over a little rise, and there facing them was Riley, or the Riley look-alike, whichever it was. He didn't say a word. He had a rifle ready, waiting for them, and fired a shot which blew Ramon's body back into Elizabeth.

Hutto dropped to his knees and rolled back against Chico, tripping him, grabbing the pistol from his hand. The mountain man fired another blast, barely missing them as they sprawled on the trail. The noise from the rifle and Elizabeth's screams echoed among the hills. Another rifle shot plowed the ground and kicked dirt into Chico's eyes. By then Hutto was scrambling away from him and firing at the man with the rifle. The second shot put a hole in the center of his chest.

Elizabeth, still screaming, was covered with pieces of Ramon. Chico was scratching at his eyes with one hand and digging for the daypack with the other, so Hutto dived back onto him, clipped him hard behind the ear with the pistol barrel, and ripped the daypack off him. Standing there with the weight of its weapons balanced in one hand and the hot pistol in the other, he kicked Chico in the ribs and thought about giving him another ear hole.

Then Elizabeth started making noise again and he turned to see the Riley look-alike struggling to his knees. So he fired another shot, which bored into the big man's gut. He flopped onto his back and moaned.

Hutto ran up to him, bent over, and looked into his eyes. They weren't yet glazed, still alive, still fierce.

"Talk," Hutto said.

For an answer, the mountain man spit at him.

"Who are you?" Hutto asked.

"Billy."

The man belched up his name, fighting for breath.

"Got my daddy," Billy said. "Got my daddy, got Axe, got me now."

"You're the brother, then."

Billy looked up at him with eyes like Philip's when he died in the cave.

"Forgot about you," Hutto said. "You were sick when Axel and I met. That's what he said."

"Stomach flu," Billy said.

"Lucky," Hutto said. "You got to live one more day."

He backed off a couple of feet, pointed the pistol at Billy's forehead, and pulled the trigger. The body jumped, jerked, convulsed. Riley's seed dies hard, Hutto thought.

Elizabeth was on the ground vomiting. It seemed the echoes from the gunshots bounced on and on through the mountains, ringing from peak to peak to valley and back, but maybe it was just Hutto's ears ringing.

Hutto took off his pack and sat in the middle of the trail, listening to Elizabeth's sobs. Chico didn't move. Hutto couldn't tell if he was knocked out or pretending. After a few minutes Elizabeth stopped crying, started cleaning herself as well as possible, and noticed Hutto watching the Colombian.

"Kill him," she said.

"I'm thinking."

"Kill him now."

"I'm thinking about it, damn it."

"You never listen to anybody."

"That's right," he said.

She moved off the trail about fifty feet to a rhododendron thicket and stared off into the reddening sky.

"Let's leave this stuff and get out of here," she finally said.

"Can't do it."

"You're alive. That ought to be enough."

"Can't do it."

"Why the hell not?"

"I want to finish it," he said.

"This isn't a finish?"

"Not even close."

"Looks finished to me."

"No way."

"You're weird," she said. "Too weird for words."

"Maybe I am a little different. But not weird. Weird is when you're just downright nasty."

"Look around you. That's not nasty enough?"

"That's kind of gory, but it couldn't be helped. That's just life."

"Just life."

"Yeah. And death. It's natural."

"Hutto, you need a brain transplant."

"Maybe I do. That's not a bad idea."

After a while Chico's left leg started twitching, and then his right leg started. He flexed his fingers, stretched his arms, and sat up, jiggling his head.

"Wake-up call," Hutto said.

Elizabeth ran up the hill. "Kill him," she said. "I'm telling you, kill him now."

"First he's got to work," Hutto said. "Those little boys in Baranquilla learn to work hard, don't they, Chico? They tote them bales and haul that water, right? Come on, Chico, quote us some Shakespeare now."

"What's *wrong* with you?" Elizabeth asked.

"Nothing. I just want to see Chico work a little. Come on, son, get to your feet," Hutto said, aiming the pistol at the Colombian.

"Perhaps I can't," he said.

"No perhaps crap," Hutto said. "Get up."

"Wait a minute."

"Get up. Who's the fool now? Just get up, Chico."

Chico slowly pulled himself from the ground and stood. He slumped a little, feeling the back of his head.

"Time to work," Hutto said.

"I will not work for you. You'll kill me first."

"No, you'll work."

"Kill me now."

"Here we go again," Hutto said. "First I want you to kill me, and you won't. Now you want me to kill you, and *I* won't. No one accommodates anyone else anymore."

"If you don't kill me, you better watch yourself."

"Oh, shut up," Hutto said. "Christ's sake, I'm sick of this."

"Kill him," Elizabeth said. "He's right."

"You, too," Hutto said. "I don't need coaching. This isn't the Little League."

Chico stumbled a little. "Okay, what?" he said.

"Now you're talking. First, you're going to tidy up around here. I can't stand people who litter our national parks. Why don't you start with what's left of your buddy there and carry him off the trail and hide him. I mean, way off, where nobody will find him."

So Chico picked up the bloody carcass, slung it across a shoulder and moved slowly downhill. Hutto followed him, pistol in hand, wearing the daypack now. Chico buried Ramon under some leaves, a couple of rotting logs, and rocks. Then Hutto forced him to climb to the trail again, and this time carry Billy and place him next to Ramon.

"Good thing you've lifted weights," Hutto said. "Old Billy-boy here is a big one."

By the time Billy was covered, Chico was exhausted, and he sank to his hands and knees, giving Hutto time to think. If no one smelled the bodies, they'd lie there forever. Even if someone did smell them, they'd probably never find them, thinking it was a dead beast of some kind. Most likely, a persistent wild boar or maybe a bear would root them out and pick them clean.

Digging and climbing, climbing and digging, took an hour or more. When Chico could walk again, they made their way back up the Noland Divide trail, with Chico now carrying one of the packs, Hutto with the other, walking next to Elizabeth, who had the daypack.

It was dark but not so dark that Hutto couldn't see Luis limping along the trail ahead of them, coming toward them, holding his head. Hutto had figured Billy killed Luis before getting to them. Maybe he'd only knocked him out or grazed him with a bullet.

"Okay, Chico, time to talk," Hutto said. "See your buddy Luis hobbling along up there? You're going to take care of him. I know you hate his guts anyway. The Cowboys just sent him along to keep watch on you, because they don't trust you anymore, the slimy little bastard. You're the man who knows how to kill a hundred different ways, right? You're the one who can rip out a heart while the guy is still breathing, aren't you? So you take care of Luis, just you and your two hands."

"I can't do that."

"Look at it this way. Luis is going to die on this trail tonight. You can die with him, or you can live a little longer. You choose."

Chico squatted, breathing heavily. "I never liked him," he said. "You're right. He's here to watch me, just because of the quantity of coke involved."

"Let's see you do it. You don't have to hurt him."

"I suppose I have to bury him, too?"

"Absolutely. You're the prisoner here."

They walked on and met Luis at the bottom of the hill. Luis jogged a little faster to meet them, babbling in Spanish. Hutto guessed he was explaining how Billy managed to get past him despite his vigilance. He watched Chico walk to the smaller man, motioning with his hands, and then place those hands on Luis's shoulders as though all was forgiven. Then one hand slipped to the neck and the other moved to the nose and quickly, quietly, twisted.

Chico caught Luis as he fell, and turned to Hutto. "I think he felt nothing," he said.

"Does it matter?"

"Of course."

"To who?"

"To me. It's a matter of pride."

"Don't tell me about it," Hutto said. "Just hide him."

They buried Luis as they had Ramon and Billy, covering him in a small cave formed when a huge oak fell, pulling its root with it. There wasn't much trail left, and before long they were back at the parking area. The Jeep, Chico's Chevy, and the old Buick were still there. They looked in the Buick and saw the black-haired beauty asleep on the front seat.

"Kill her, too?" Elizabeth asked.

"She probably knows nothing," Chico said. "Perhaps she thinks only of making love and nothing else."

"That's a perhaps that can fry you," Elizabeth said.

"If she was an ugly old hag, would you let her go?" Chico asked. "If her breasts were tiny and shriveled, could she live? I will not kill her. I will die first."

"I wouldn't think of it," Hutto said. "Why would we want to pluck such a lovely flower?"

"I agree," Chico said. "Let's not turn our hearts to stone."

"No more poetry, Chico."

"I'm sorry. I can't help it."

"You better learn to help it."

So they turned away from the girl, letting her sleep, dreaming of the Rileys and Billys of the world, the wild men who shook her nights. But those two never would again.

Elizabeth drove the Jeep. Chico drove the Chevy as Hutto trained the pistol on him.

"That's over," Chico said.

"What's that?"

"Everything."

"Unless you kill me," Hutto said.

"Yes, that's right. But you're the brave one. You're the crazy one. In Baranquilla they'll say you killed our three best men. You'll be a legend."

"Just drive, Chico."

"Now is your opportunity to kill me. I've buried your bodies. I've carried your cocaine. You are through with me."

"Haven't you noticed, Chico, that nobody can just kill anybody any more? It's not like the old days when you could just blow people away, like Billy did. For guys like us, that's over."

"You're setting me up."

"No. I'm not. Besides, you're wrong. All the bodies aren't buried yet."

## Chapter Sixteen

Hutto kept watching Chico. A guy like that might do anything, might flick out one almost-invisible karate chop, or come up with a hidden knife, or steer the car into a tree and leap out before the impact.

Chico was probably one of the world's most honest men, if he was on your side, Hutto figured, and one of the most deadly, if he was against you. No one had ever beaten him before. That much was certain. He had to wonder why he was still alive. That was a question Hutto himself couldn't answer.

"Hutto," Chico said, starting to talk.

"Shut up."

"A civil conversation?"

"Just drive."

"I only want to talk."

"Talk can get you killed."

"What a hero, Hutto. Ramon disappears. Luis disappears. Chico mysteriously gone, without a trace."

"I quit being a hero a long time ago."

"Heroes never quit."

"If you don't shut up, you're going to get plugged right here."

"Spoken like John Wayne."

Hutto inserted the pistol barrel in Chico's ear, wiggling it just a bit. "Drive and shut up," he said.

Chico took both hands off the steering wheel and lightly waved them in the air. Hutto jammed the steel deeper, pushing for the Colombian's eardrum. Chico grunted and grabbed the wheel again. Hutto eased off.

"Gonna behave?" he asked.

"Always," Chico said, and drove on in silence, following the Jeep's taillights. They came down the mountain and passed Newfound Gap once again. The parking lot was almost empty.

"Everyone in Colombia and Miami will assume you have beaten all three of us," Chico said. "They would know all three of us would never cross them, not even me, and I'm the only one who might attempt it. So, they will toast your cunning and stay up late at night sipping margaritas, worrying about how to catch you. You'll be an epic hero of sorts, the legendary bad man."

"Great. Now I'll have to fret about every South American I see."

"And every Swede and Texan and Asian and African. It takes a very bad man to catch one so great as Hutto, and bad men come in all colors and sizes."

"I'm looking forward to it."

"It'll be an honor to track you, their fiercest enemy. They are primitive enough to enjoy this sort of thing."

"Like the Indians who ate the hearts of their enemies."

"What's that?"

"Some American Indians ate their enemies' hearts."

"To take their courage?"

"Yeah. To be legendary bad men in their own way."

"An interesting Stone Age concept."

"We still have some with us."

"How do you know this?"

"Riley was one."

"Riley?"

"You know. Our friend Billy's father."

"The wild man with the hair and beard?"

"Right. He caught tourists for a hobby. He enjoyed the women, and God knows what he did with the men. He robbed them, and did his thing, and then ate their hearts. He almost ate mine and Elizabeth's."

"It's a way of honoring you."

"I can do without that kind of honor."

"What honor do you intend for me?" Chico asked.

"Something fitting."

"Such as?"

"Such as letting you take the heat from your friends in Colombia, while I disappear."

201

"I resist heat quite well."

"Until now."

"I don't think anyone can turn the burner up hot enough to scorch me."

"How about this scenario? Luis was loyal, proud to have the job watching you. Ramon was on the way up, ready to take your place. Whereas I'm just a dumb gringo who got in over his head. So you kill me, kill your buddies, and then sell the stuff yourself."

"Nobody will believe that."

"They will when you turn up in Miami spending money like a wealthy man."

"I won't turn up in Miami. Anyway, I can easily explain what happened."

"That I beat you? How can you explain that? Either way, you're a goner. If they think you ripped them off, they'll kill you. If they think I beat you, they'll still kill you."

"If I did rip them off, I'd never go to Miami."

"That's what they'd think you'd want them to think. That's exactly why you'd go there, and I'll be right with you."

"Preposterous, Hutto. It makes no sense at all," Chico said, looking out the side window at the black outline of the mountains against the evening sky.

Hutto was thinking fast, making this up as he went along. He never figured on having Chico on his hands.

"Ripping them off didn't make sense in the first

place," he said. "They'll think you've gone crazy for sure."

"At least let me die with honor, Hutto."

"What honor?"

"Not as a double-crosser. Not as a fool would die."

"Why should I care how you die? You want me to kill you here?"

"Correct."

"Naw. Too easy, Chico."

"We could make a deal."

Now Hutto laughed. "No deals, Chico," he said.

"You wanted to deal earlier."

"That's when you held the gun."

"I can offer you a number of services vital to keeping you alive. You'll be a marked man now. That's what I was trying to explain. Everybody will want your blood. You have little chance of surviving long. The world is a small place, Hutto. No matter where you go, death will wait."

"Death waits for us all, Chico."

"I can help stall it."

"I doubt it. First time I set you loose, you'd kill me and go running back to Colombia."

Chico shook his head and pounded the steering wheel with a fist.

"Even if you did set me free, I think Colombia is no longer my home. As you say, the Cowboys would never believe my story. If you defeat me, I'm as good as dead. If I return without the cocaine, it's the same, and so much of it is already gone thanks to the bear and the elements."

"My heart aches for you, Chico."

"Do not belittle others, my friend."

"That's what you get when you throw in with guys like the Cowboys. You're belittled right from the start. Only you don't know it, until it's too late."

"I had no choice."

"No. Free men have choices."

"It's been many years since I was a free man."

"Everybody's free. If you don't want to do what the bad boys want, you just stick that pistol in your ear and bang, you're free."

"You don't understand."

"I understand all too well, Chico. If you had any courage, you'd have killed yourself years ago."

"Still, I don't want this humiliation and death in Miami. Perhaps you could let me have the pistol now, and I'd do the job."

"Are you nuts? No pistols for you, Chico."

"And no deals?"

"I have no reason to deal with you."

"And if I gave you a reason?"

"It'd have to be a good one."

"I'll think on it."

"You do that. Just keep your eye on the road. You're so worked up you keep running in the ditch. We wouldn't want to have an accident."

## Chapter Seventeen

"What about the girl?" Chico asked. "Does she live through this?"

Hutto looked at Elizabeth up ahead, seeing her silhouette in the Jeep as she steered it down the mountain.

"Chico, you surprise me," Hutto said. He inserted the barrel of the pistol in Chico's right ear again. "How would you like a connecting tunnel between your ears?"

"Not so much," he said. "It's just that women worry me."

"Your worries are about over, anyhow."

"If she follows you, yours are just starting. Women cause trouble. Women and money, that's double trouble."

"I don't see how it's any concern of yours."

"Maybe not. I can see trouble coming, Hutto. See, I have studied you, as I study all my assignments. I understand you. I know what made you the way you are."

"You don't know crap, Chico."

"I feel a sort of kinship with you."

"Because you were going to kill me? You're weird."

"This girl has a meanness to her you don't see. Like back there when she wanted to kill the black-haired girl. Her eyes showed it. That could destroy you."

"She was just excited and scared. She's no fool."

"Don't take her side just because she's a female and ready and willing to breed. You sniff the air behind her like a bull trailing a heifer in heat."

"It's not the same. She's not even my girl," Hutto said.

"She is now. No piece of paper can tie you stronger than you already are. She'll resent it. It'll make her hate you. One day, she makes a phone call, or drops a postcard into the mail, or even just winks her eye just so, and you fall dead. A herd of bad men comes running. They kill you, get the money, and keep the girl for a reward."

"I don't think so."

"What do you know about her, if she's not your girl?"

"Everything I need to know. You ought to know that, you're the guy with all the personal information."

"She's going to be a problem," Chico said.

"You've got problems enough of your own. Don't worry about mine."

"You could kill her. You could kill me. Then you could be on your own, totally free for a time."

"What happened to your ethics, Chico? Killing you wouldn't bother me. Killing her, now that's something else again. I couldn't sleep nights after that. My mind would be in prison, even if my body was free."

"I don't think you can do it, Hutto. What if I forced you to shoot right now?"

"I'd shoot."

"Perhaps not. You can shoot in battle, but not as a murderer. There's a big difference."

"Try me."

"The Cowboys would do it without hesitation."

"I'm not the Cowboys. And you won't be in the club much longer yourself."

"You think you're smarter than them. Stronger. A good guy. You have no loose ends, you think. Nothing can snag you."

Hutto looked at Elizabeth up ahead, combing her hair with her fingers, looking at herself in the rearview mirror. "I'm just doing the best I can," he said.

"You can't make this work. They're not so dumb. If they kill me in Miami, they'll find no money. They'll find no cocaine. They'll wonder why Chico was such a fool. I've always been careful. That's why I survived so long. Why would I do all this just to turn up in Miami?"

"Let 'em wonder about it."

"They'll still be after you. They don't need telephone books and the FBI to track you. They'll find you. You won't even hear them coming. Then, poof, it's all over for you."

"I'll handle it."

"Foolish confidence."

"Shut up, Chico."

"You need me."

"Shut up, Chico."

"You do."

Hutto popped Chico lightly on the back of the head with the pistol, then stuck the barrel back in his ear. "I don't need a single living soul, Chico. That includes you. Shut up before I clean out your ear wax."

But Chico wouldn't be quiet. "There's a way out of this," he said. "There's always a way, if you know how to look."

"No deals, Chico."

"Fine. I won't trouble you again."

"I appreciate it."

They rode on, easing down the mountain. The Jeep's taillights glowed red in the darkness. Occasionally, on the side of the road, there'd be a woodchuck or some other creature slipping through the night.

"So you beat them," Chico said.

"I said to shut up."

"Well, say, theoretically, that you beat them. You escape this country. They're not stupid, but they're not geniuses, either, so it could be done. What they are is rich, rich beyond any riches you can conceive of. And scared. They're always scared of losing their money. They don't trust each other. They fight amongst themselves. Which one will be boss now? Things like that. Always the infighting. They're scared of dying. Of losing those beautiful young women of theirs who do whatever they want. Like wild dogs in a pack, they are vicious. Alone, some are cowards. Some are not. They're all full of fear, in their way. They are all afraid of me, because I do this work they fear. Every one. That makes the man who kills me a superman."

"I'm not going to kill you. They are."

"I don't think so. I think it's you, if it's anyone. It is for you to decide."

"Paint an *S* on my chest."

"And a target on your heart."

"What about you? Talk about idiots, why didn't you kill me? You could have popped me, then taken Elizabeth easy enough. You could have all the money, everything."

"I'm a soldier. I do a job and go home. They pat me on the head, toss me a few dollars, give me their old girlfriends, and we're all happy. I kill who they want killed. I do what I must."

"So you owe them something. They got you out of that prison, so you're sort of a slave now. Were you guilty the first time?"

"Yes, of course."

"You just have the killer bred into you?"

"If you say so. But that first man needed killing. He mistreated my mother. He was her lover. He hurt her. I killed him. It was simple. Since that day, she hates me. It is another of life's mysteries."

Chico had an excuse for everything. Hutto didn't like that. He'd never cared for drunks who explained away their problem by blaming fathers who were alcoholics, or child abusers who claimed they did it because they'd been abused themselves, or people who blamed their poor self-image on parents who didn't appreciate them. Everybody stands alone in this world, Hutto thought. You can't lean on anything. No excuses. He'd like that to be branded on the brain of every human on earth.

He thought about that, not really listening as the Colombian continued babbling about his mother and how much he had wanted to be a schoolteacher before killing his first man, getting trapped into the life of a professional killer. Hutto leaned on the dashboard of the rented Chevy and pointed the pistol directly at Chico's nose, using it to emphasize every word.

"You could have quit any day, if they're as afraid of you as you say. You could have put the brakes on the whole damn thing. If they went ahead and killed you, you'd have done the moral and right thing. The deal is, you had to have liked it. You had to have liked having the power to let people live or let them die. I think you liked the idea of ridding the world of its pests. You think you're the guy on the white horse. You're some piece of work, Chico. Your mind is going off in twenty directions at once justifying your life."

"I try not to be idle."

What a crazy bastard, Hutto thought. He looked

at the pistol and sighted down the barrel into the darkness. This little piece of metal here sure can solve problems, he thought, remembering how Billy had gone down back on the trail.

Of course, it can cause a few, too.

## Chapter Eighteen

Gatlinburg burned dully in the night, a little windup tourist town slapped into the wild hills. Elizabeth drove by the convention center and headed for Burger King. Waiting in the Chevy, Hutto and Chico saw teenagers everywhere, flirting, gossiping, doing whatever it is they do these days. Hutto wondered how much of his cocaine these lanky young hotshots had stuffed up their noses. If any of this particular load ever hit the streets of their towns, they'd never know how many people died to give them that little kick.

Elizabeth came out with a bag of burgers, didn't say a word, got in the Jeep, and drove up the steep road toward the chalet. Chico kept turning in his seat to look at things, at the House of Tomorrow plunked down like a warped marshmallow on a weedy lot, at the dinosaurs in the putt-putt golf course, at people dressed like clowns who were actually trying to con tourists into buying time-share condos.

"I don't understand this place," he said.

"Join the crowd. I think hell is just a big place with absolutely nothing to do but play putt-putt golf."

They followed the Jeep up the mountain. Elizabeth took the curves too fast and wide. Chico drove carefully and hung with her. A few cars came from the other direction, descending from the ski lodge. Ober Gatlinburg pretended to be a German establishment magically dropped into Appalachia. An oompah band, decked out in lederhosen, pranced on a platform in the dining room during ski season, but the real partiers hung out in the dark bar hidden to the side, listening to loud rock music, pretending to be worldly. Hutto used to go there for beer and to look at a redheaded waitress who kept his attention for a few months. She took his tips, but that was all.

Now, though, in midsummer, the ski lodge closed early. Few other than the most curious made it that far into the mountains. Some rode the aerial tram to the top for what passed for adventure, and some came to look at the black bears kept there to attract summer tourists.

Just before they got to the chalet, Hutto flashed his headlights. Elizabeth stopped, walked back to his side of the Chevy, and stood there. Hutto stared at the triangular-shaped building, looking for a sign. Nothing moved. Nothing offered a target. Everything seemed normal. Hutto couldn't hear any birds or crickets or katydids, and vaguely wondered why.

He didn't want to be surprised twice this day, so he got out of the car holding the pistol. She touched his hand, then held his arm near the elbow. Chico opened his door and got out of the car. Hutto motioned for him to walk in front, and he did, looking like he was strolling the grounds at an outdoor party.

Hutto began to sweat. His stomach churned. He wasn't sure what to do with Chico. Even when Hutto had the gun, Chico seemed too calm, too sure, too talkative. He wondered about the cops. What if they were in there waiting? One night to go, a few lousy hours, and suddenly the cops get wise? Or, the Italians decide to skip tomorrow's little ritual and get it over with tonight?

Keeping his eyes on Chico, he moved to the door, listening. Nothing.

Now Chico seemed tense, too, and stood crouched. He sniffed the air, like a dog. Hutto wondered if he could smell death waiting.

Then Hutto quietly put the key in the door and swung it open. He pushed Chico ahead of him. Chico grunted, "Hey!" and tripped over the doorway, going to his knees. When he did, whoever was inside fired a gun with a blinding flash in the darkness.

Hutto jumped back from the door, shoved Elizabeth toward the woods, and ran after her. He heard a couple more shots, wondered if they were for him or Chico, and reached deep within his body for more speed. Elizabeth was still ahead, crashing through the undergrowth, and he wanted to catch her before she got too far out front and got lost or killed.

Then, stumbling, he hit a tree face-first and slammed onto his back, stunned. Elizabeth ran back, found him, grabbed his pistol, whipped around, fired, and a dead man fell over them.

She pushed the body to the side and held Hutto's head.

"Where'd he shoot you?" she asked.

"Ran into a tree."

"You're not shot?"

"I don't think so."

"You ran into a damn tree?"

"You got it."

"I wonder if you're worth saving."

"I'll prove it. Later."

Hutto sat up on his knees, jiggling his nose. Not broken, but sore. He could feel a little warm blood trickling down his forehead, then saw the dark stain on his hand.

The dead guy was little, five-five at the most. He wore new blue jeans, a Hard Rock Cafe T-shirt, and had a pair of Nike running shoes on his feet. Hutto got down close so he could see in the darkness and looked at the face, then reached around for the guy's wallet. He had some ID in there, and

Hutto flipped through it, thinking about what he saw.

"This guy's no cop," he said.

"Thank God for that."

"I give you five to one he's Colombian."

"Uh-oh. Bad news?"

"It's not good."

"They're gong to just keep coming for us, aren't they?"

"Looks like it."

It didn't make a lot of sense, though. The Colombians had no way of knowing yet that Hutto had gotten the jump on Chico. For all they knew, Chico was still tracking them down. They wouldn't kill Chico, because he was still their man, and they wouldn't kill Hutto, because he could lead them to the coke. Something wasn't right. Hutto slowly rose to his feet, rubbing his head.

"Where are you going?" Elizabeth asked.

"Back to the chalet."

"Are you nuts?"

He shrugged. They walked back uphill, Hutto in the lead. The chalet sat there, dark and silent. The Jeep and Chevy were still parked on the roadside. Nothing moved.

Hutto didn't like killing people.

But it beat being killed.

There'd be some more killing, one way or the other, before this night ended.

Like Chico said, face-to-face, Hutto couldn't do

much, but in a battle, he could become a killing machine. The old instincts, learned at Fort Bragg, Fort Benning, and the Southeast Asian jungle, never died. They just waited for the right moment to revive.

Now was the time.

He came to the edge of the clearing and motioned Elizabeth to stay behind. She shook her head no. Yes, he mouthed. Stay here.

No. She shook her head and pointed back toward where the dead Colombian lay, cocking a finger and pretending to shoot. He couldn't deny that she'd gotten off a hell of a shot that saved him back there, so she came on, following so close she might have been a shadow, if there'd been light enough for shadows.

They ran to the back of the chalet, under the deck, and listened. Silence. Then, along the side of the chalet. Still silence. Hutto moved forward until he was kneeling directly under the window of the living room, not far from the front door.

Somebody in there moved. A foot scraped softly on the floor. A nose sniffed. Hutto thought he could hear heavy breathing, and somebody—Chico maybe—moaning a little. Then a voice, soft and low, the kind of voice the devil might use calling you down to his putt-putt golf course.

A voice, speaking Spanish. Two words. He couldn't understand them. "Let's go?" "Give up?" "You die?" He didn't know.

He knew they were waiting on the guy with the Nikes. But they wouldn't wait long. If they came out to look for him, Hutto could blast them as they came off the porch. They'd have to come out soon, and he could wait as long as they could.

Then there was a noise, like the heavens' loudest thunder, an explosion, an incredible roar within the chalet. Hutto thought they might have had a bomb of some sort and accidentally set it off. The door blew open, and first one, then two, black Japanese motorcycles shot through the opening and landed in the driveway. They didn't hesitate, only accelerated, kicking gravel, to the road and uphill, up the mountain, away into the night. Hutto saw Chico sitting behind one of the drivers, slumped in the big banana seat, roped onto the bike.

Elizabeth ran up, watching them go.

"What now?" she asked.

"Now we go after them," Hutto said, running for the Jeep. "Come on, come on, we have to finish it."

She barely got to the passenger seat when he started up the mountain road, driving without lights. The motorcycles made so much noise they could hear them even over the Jeep engine. There weren't many places they could go. Going uphill like this, they either had to go to a chalet, which Hutto somehow doubted, or they'd go to the ski lodge. He couldn't imagine why they'd do that, but those were their only two choices. They couldn't very well head downhill and cruise through Gatlinburg with Chico tied and probably bleeding on the back of his bike.

"Just let them have Chico," Elizabeth yelled. "Who cares?"

"This is for us," he said. "If we don't finish it now, we'll always be wondering when they'll come riding upon those bikes hunting *us*."

The motorcycles went up as far as they could go, then climbed the steep grade into the ski lodge parking lot. Hutto stopped the Jeep at the foot and peeked over the rise.

There they were, parked by the hut where the ski patrol hung out during the winter season. Hutto could have picked them both off with a rifle. Could have picked all three of them off. These two new ones, and his good friend Chico, who'd probably do the same for him if he had the opportunity.

They were sitting there, still on the bikes, waiting, he guessed, to see if anyone was going to follow them. He slid back down to the Jeep.

"Well?" she said.

"You've got to help."

"Save Chico?"

"Save us. You've got to do it this once."

"I've already done it, whatever it is, several times this week."

"We have to hurry. I'm going to sneak up on these guys, but I need a distraction. I don't think they really know who you are. They may know me, but not you. Something tells me it's Chico they want and we're secondary. So listen up. This is your big chance."

She listened. She didn't like what he said, but she listened, and she agreed to the plan. She started counting when he got out of the Jeep. When she reached 100 she slid out herself, started singing in a drunken slur and ambled crookedly up the little hill to the edge of the parking lot.

She was supposed to be drunk, but all she felt was fear. She couldn't think of any songs, couldn't remember the words to one, not a hymn or a country song. So she made up her own. Somehow she had always wanted to be a songwriter. English was her best subject in school. She didn't think she could sit down and write a book, but she figured she could get through a song, and she had a little talent for it. When she was with a man who owned a piano she used to sit down and pick out songs she heard on the radio. That kind of amazed her, knowing she could do it. Sometimes she went to Nashville and listened to the great songwriters at the Bluebird Cafe, to Paul Overstreet and Don Schlitz and Thom Schuyler and Gary Nicholson. She had seen Dean Dillon and Guy Clark and Russell Smith and Marshall Chapman. It was too late for her now, of course, but if things had gone right, if life had a little more rhyme and reason, she could have been up there, playing a Yamaha DX-7 piano, strumming a guitar, singing her new hit songs.

As it was, she had never written a song. She just didn't know what to do with one. But now came the first, a song she made up walking to what could be her end. She stepped to the edge of the parking lot, wondering when the shot would take off the top of her head. She was singing now as loud as she could.

"Here's to you old Tennessee, your mountains look good to me; They're rising high, right up to the sky, and they set your soul plumb free."

She took a breath, staggering around a bit like a drunk might, and wiped some sweat from her face, still listening for that shot.

"Well I take a drink for me; and I take a drink for you; nobody here cares if you take a drink or two."

She looked up at the ski patrol hut as she twirled around. The Colombians were watching her, gesturing, saying something to each other. Come on, damn you. Come on, she thought. Come on, let's get it over with.

"We've got corn in the ground and corn in the bottle; Yeah, all that corn just hits my throttle, and then blows right on through."

The one sitting along on the motorcycle eased forward a few yards, considering what to do.

She staggered on, moving toward the lodge, wondering what she'd do if neither of them made a move for her, wondering where Hutto was, if he'd gotten into position yet, if it'd work out the way he said it would. Then she knew it wouldn't. Of course not. Did anything?

"Everybody says it's a good place to find love; well, too much love still ain't enough, and that's why your hills are so blue."

The one out front moved toward her, slowly, cautiously, looking back at his buddy as he did. She shook her hair around and around, trying to look wild, drunk, and crazy.

"Listen to that fiddle music and pass it on around; when you're so far up you'll never get down, and you can sing a song that's true."

Here he came, slowly, slowly. She could see his face now, could see he was older than she'd figured a guy on a motorcycle would be, could see him grinning. He thinks he's going to knock off an easy piece, she thought.

"Yeah, here's to you old Tennessee, your mountains look so good to me; they're rising high, right up to the sky, and they set your soul plumb free."

Then, there he was, and she was wondering where Hutto was when she really needed him.

"Hello, there," she said. "Big guy on a bike. Great night to get drunk and go for a walk, huh?"

He sat there, ten feet away now, idling the engine, watching her. "Want to go for a ride?" he said, sounding a lot like Chico but with a heavier accent.

"I love to walk at night," she said, slurring her words.

"Riding is also quite romantic," he said.

"You look like a romantic guy."

"Quite," he said. "My ladies say I'm the best. Maybe you would like to try me."

Then she heard a loud pop from up around the shed and saw Hutto struggling with the other Colombian, pulling him off the bike. Chico just flopped over with the machine and lay there.

This one turned on his bike and saw what was happening. He looked at her, shook his head, and swooped upon her, flipping her over the fuselage of the bike in front of him. Damn Hutto, she thought, struggling to free herself. Damn him, he wasn't supposed to let the guy get this close.

Then she heard a deafening roar over her head and realized the guy was shooting at Hutto, so she tried hitting at his hand to make him miss, but he just popped her a solid chop across the back of the head with the hot pistol, and that's all she saw or felt for awhile.

Hutto had unexpected trouble creeping around behind the hut. The ground was more open than he'd thought it would be, and there was more of it to cover than he'd remembered. By the time he got into position, the first Colombian was already near Elizabeth. Then when he'd fired at the one on the bike with Chico, the guy rolled back just enough that the shot missed. So he'd jumped him, pulled him down off the bike, and finally got his pistol in position to plant a bullet in his ear.

By then, though, the other one had Elizabeth on his bike and was heading off behind the lodge, probably figuring Hutto and Elizabeth had reinforcements on the way. Chico was just lying there in the parking lot like a sack of flour. Hutto wondered if he was alive. He'd check it later.

He hopped on the motorcycle, starting it. Good thing it didn't flood when it fell over as they scuffled, he thought. He turned to follow them, but it had been a long time since he'd ridden a motorcycle, and this one got away from him. It jumped powerfully forward, and ran right over the Colombian he'd just shot, dumping Hutto onto the asphalt.

He picked himself up and got going again. By this time the Colombian and Elizabeth were far ahead, charging right up the ski slope. There were several runs here, all shooting off from one main slope. He saw the guy's bike bouncing along in the darkness, running without lights, swerving and jumping as it struggled with the weight of two people.

The Colombian turned right on the first run, Cub-way. Hutto had always wondered why anybody would name a ski run Cub-way. He slammed along behind the Colombian and turned, making up a little ground. The Colombian had an extra load on his bike, and he was hitting the bumps hard, losing time.

Cub-way wasn't all that tough, if you were any

kind of skier at all. Going up it in the darkness on the motorcycle was harder than going down it on skis, though. He saw the Colombian stop and turn to watch him, saw him raise an arm and fire a pistol at him. But he knew it was next to impossible to hit anything firing down at such a steep angle, so he didn't hesitate, just pushed the bike harder, upward, and onward.

The Colombian kept going where Cub-way branches off from a run called Edelweiss. The ride got harder here and more vertical. Hutto wondered what the Colombian thought he was doing. He could go up, up, up and die at the top, or he could turn around and die at the bottom. People tend to go up when they're in danger. They climb a tree when they're chased, rather than keep running well ahead of the pursuit. Maybe it's the monkey in us. We revert to what we were a few million years ago, swinging in the trees with a grasping tail.

Every now and then the Colombian would stop and shoot at him a time or two. Hutto figured he must have several clips with him, wasting ammo like that. By now he had to be tired of hauling Elizabeth around. She was going to be a sore woman tomorrow. Nobody could bounce that hard face down on a motorcycle and not feel it the next day.

Hutto was much closer now. He could hear the roar of the other motorcycle and even see the guy's eyes as he turned around to fire another shot at him. They twisted around, back and forth up Edelweiss, then came to the point where Edelweiss joins a trail called Mogul Ridge, and pushed on. In a couple of minutes the Colombian whipped left down a run called Grizzly. Now he was going downhill, almost literally straight down the kind of hill all but the most expert skiers slowly traverse back and forth to keep from toppling on their heads. But the Colombian didn't know Grizzly made a loop of sorts, and that the Mogul Ridge run went directly down the mountain.

Hutto knew, though, and when the Colombian moved onto Grizzly, he turned back, flying down Mogul Ridge, ready to meet the guy when he came to the bottom. Mogul Ridge was well named. Every time Hutto got up to speed he hit another tremendous bump and several times almost bounced off the bike. But he always somehow came down on two tires and went scrambling away.

It was a hard ride, wild and tough. When he got to the point toward the bottom of the mountain where Grizzly joins Mogul Ridge, there was no Colombian in sight, and no Elizabeth. He backed into a stand of trees and waited under cover, out of sight. Then he heard them.

The bike slowed as they got to the place where the runs branched. Hutto eased forward, pulling out his pistol, wondering how to shoot the Colombian without shooting Elizabeth.

The Colombian saw him and stopped the bike to

get a solid shot off. He rested one hand almost tenderly on Elizabeth's back. Then Elizabeth rolled off the bike backwards, slapping at her captor, pushing his hand aside. He looked at Hutto, then looked at Elizabeth on the ground, thinking about which of them to shoot first.

The gun lowered at Elizabeth, and Hutto fired. He missed.

The guy looked up then, glaring at Hutto. Without taking aim he snapped a shot which chipped the seat just forward from where Hutto sat.

Hutto wheeled the bike to the side a few feet, aimed, fired, and missed again. This time the Colombian wouldn't miss. Hutto could feel it. So he revved the motorcycle, popped the wheel, and roared forward, charging the guy like an Arthurian knight, waving the pistol like a lance.

He yelled.

The yell grew into a high-pitched scream like the Rebel yell that filled the battlefield air during the Civil War. He flew across the space separating them, swerving, dodging where he imagined the Colombian would be shooting—barely missed Elizabeth lying there—and caught the guy before he could get going again. He dove off the bike and hauled the Colombian to the ground.

The Colombian was hitting at him with his pistol but Hutto felt nothing. He was too busy hitting, too, feeling the metal bite skin. Then, tired of this, weary of too much death and too many senseless killing, but resigned to at least one more, he knocked the Colombian's hand to the side and kicked the pistol away.

He held his own pistol two inches from the tip of the Colombian's nose. They stayed that way ten seconds. Then the Colombian decided he'd let his sweet personality get him out of this.

"What's wrong with you, man?" he said. "She is just a girl. We get lots of girls. I get you another if this one is damaged."

"What are you doing here?" Hutto asked.

The Colombian looked at him, weighing his chances, considering the possibilities. "Ricky sent us," he said.

"Ricky?"

"You don't know Ricky? He knows you."

"Ricky who?"

"Guzman. Who else?"

"Guzman, huh? Ricardo Guzman, the semi-big shot."

"Oh, he is a big shot all the way, now. We had a little, what you call it? A coup? Yes, a little war. Ricky is number one now. The old big shots are dead or gone or in jail. It's Ricky now. He's in charge."

"What's that have to do with us?"

"Ricky has some business to discuss with Chico, and you have something that belongs to Ricky. I'm just minding my own business up here, and you come along chasing me and this drunk girl. We just want a little romance, why you have to make trouble?"

"You were born for trouble, boy."

"I don't understand."

"Tell me, have you ever played putt-putt golf?"

"What is this, poot-poot goof?"

"You'll find out," Hutto said, pulling back just a little. He stuck the pistol barrel in the Colombian's mouth and pulled the trigger. Somehow he didn't even hear the noise.

He slowly rose, walked a few feet away, and threw up.

Elizabeth was on her feet now and had watched the finish. She went to where he was bent over heaving, and leaned on his back. She ran a hand through his hair and held his forehead.

"You poor thing," she said. "You poor thing."

## Chapter Nineteen

Chico was sitting up, swaying slightly from side to side, still loosely tied to the fallen motorcycle. He was looking at the dead Colombian lying on the asphalt a few feet away, when Hutto and Elizabeth rounded the ski patrol hut and walked to the parking lot.

"You are hell in a battle," he said.

"Are you okay?" Hutto asked.

"One hell of a warrior."

"Ready to go? Can you stand up?"

"I don't know."

"What'd they do to you, anyway?"

"I'm not sure. They weren't very good at it, whatever it was."

Elizabeth tried to find out what was wrong with him as Hutto ran down for the Jeep. "Whose side are you on?" she asked.

Chico laughed. "My side," he said.

"Which side are we on?"

"You decide that."

Hutto jumped from the Jeep carrying his knife and slit the rope. Chico flexed and stretched.

"We're leaving here and leaving in a hurry, so don't try anything, okay?" Hutto said.

"You and I are of one mind," Chico said.

"You have to tell me about Ricky."

"Later. Let's go while I can."

Hutto helped him to the Jeep and dumped him inside. Elizabeth held the door open. "Are we going to just leave the bodies?" she asked.

"What would you suggest?" Hutto asked her.

"Somebody will find them, won't they?"

"We'll be long gone by then. They'll never connect them to us. Besides, I've buried enough bodies today already."

"Well, somebody will have a hell of a surprise tomorrow," she said.

"And a couple of new motorcycles if they want them," Hutto said.

"Move it," Chico yelled. "Don't be fools. Just go."

So they did, roaring down the mountain toward the chalet. This time they used the headlights. They helped Chico inside. He was recovering little by little, standing almost straight now, grunting when he moved, but otherwise showing little effect of his battle. He stretched out on the couch in the living room, breathing hard.

"Bastards," he said. "Dirty bastards."

"Now you know how it feels," Hutto said. "It

sort of ruins your day when somebody sneaks up on you, trying to kill you when you're not ready."

"I'd never do it that way. I'd be efficient. I'd be more humane. I don't care for terror or horror. I just get the job done."

"Maybe, but you're out of work now. That's what it sounds like," Hutto said.

"True."

"Want to talk about it?"

"No. But considering the circumstances, I will."

Elizabeth sat on the floor, looking up at both men. "I don't get it," she said. "We've got Colomians killing Colombians. Americans killing Americans. Americans killing Colombians and who knows what all else."

"It's a long story," Chico said.

"Make it short," Hutto said.

"Okay, short version. And this is mostly what I picked up from those two, and our conversation was rather hurried, you understand. I have my bosses. You know them, Hutto. Leon was number one for some time. And then we had Carlos and Jesus under him. Further down, several management types, including Ricardo Guzman, sometimes called Ricky the Rat. Ricky was good at certain things, like dealing with politicians, both Columbian and yours here in the U.S. He could smooth the troubled waters, so to speak. He had a place and a purpose. He wanted to be top dog, though, and everybody knew it. Leon kept him on just for his skill at politics.

"Carlos sent me after you when you started your little adventure. Things were already quite tense in Baranquilla, and that's why they sent Luis and Ramon with me, to make sure I performed properly. Apparently shortly after I left Colombia, Ricky Guzman somehow pulled off a revolution within the organization. He killed Leon and Carlos. Jesus managed to escape, but is in jail in Venezuela. Ricky wanted me killed, too, I suppose, because of my reputation. He thought I could not be trusted by his new regime, which is correct. He wanted me brought home, though, so he could interrogate me and make certain I had been killed. And Ricky needed either your cocaine or the money from it to help finance his new operations. So these three came to capture me, kill you, and steal your prize. There you have it."

"How did they know about the chalet?"

"I report in. You didn't know that?"

"You mean you call back and say you're in such and such a place and here's what's going on?"

"Sure. There's a person at the office there, a woman, who tracks the location of all the operations. When I'm out on a job, she knows where I am. When someone is working, she follows their movements."

"I didn't know that. I thought you were running around out here on your own."

"No, we're more organized than that. In case

something goes wrong, they want to know where I am, where my target is, what can be done if a second operation is needed."

"So you called and told them about the chalet?"

"Of course. As soon as that plane crashed, we knew approximately where you were. All I had to do was come and track you. The Jeep was easy to spot and I knew you wouldn't check into a hotel. It's interesting, Hutto, that you've survived in this business so long and know so little about it."

"So what happens when those three guys don't report in?"

"They'll probably give them the night to do their job. If by noon tomorrow they haven't called, they'll most likely send some more men from Miami or Colombia. But without me they're a little shorthanded on specialists."

"With you and Ramon gone, they're hurting for hired guns?"

"Something like that. The apprentice program is sadly lacking."

"But somebody will be on the way."

"Without a doubt," Chico said.

"If it's not before noon tomorrow, we're safe. We'll be gone by then."

Hutto went to the refrigerator and came back with three candy bars and some potato chips.

"Care for dinner?" he asked.

After a couple of bites, Chico started laughing quietly to himself. "Those guys were so afraid of you, I thought they were going to dirty their diapers before they got out of the house on those motorcycles," he said. "I think they believed I had already killed you. Then when we came back here, and I was obviously your prisoner, they didn't know what to think. What happened to the one who ran after you?"

"He's lying down there in the woods. I ran into a tree and it nearly knocked me out. So while I'm laid out on the ground, Elizabeth grabs my pistol and drills him."

"It's nice to have a partner, is it not?"

"That's what I've been trying to tell you all along," Hutto said. "Are you in with us or not?"

"In. Is there a choice?"

Chico decided to sleep on the couch. He kept two pistols at his side and had a clear shot at the door if anyone tried to enter the chalet. Hutto watched him settle down on a couple of throw pillows and turned toward the bedroom, putting an arm around Elizabeth's shoulders.

"I'm sick and tired of all this shoot-em-up stuff," she said.

"Kept you alive, hasn't it?"

"People shouldn't have to live like this. Or die like this."

"After tomorrow, we won't any more."

"Yeah, and who dies tomorrow? Somebody dies every day, either Wilson or Riley or Ramon or the bear. Who's it going to be tomorrow? Me? You?

Mister Wonderful lying there?"

"Tomorrow will finish it."

"Chico doesn't like me, does he?"

"I think it's more that he doesn't trust women."

"He likes boys, then."

"No, I don't think so. I think he's sort of celibate, like a priest or something. He doesn't trust anybody, but especially not women."

"Like a priest, huh? For the god of death."

"Everybody finds a way to get by," Hutto said. "His way is to be purer than anyone else, because the job he does is so dirty. But I think he's involuntarily retired now."

"They'll really kill him?"

"You saw those guys. They can't trust him."

"They think he'll try to take over the outfit himself."

"Something like that, I guess."

Hutto sat on the bed. Elizabeth pulled her shirt off and slipped out of her jeans. He liked watching her and wondered if she was aware of performing for him.

She had brown skin, tanned except for the part where her bikini shielded her from the sun. Her breasts were perfect for her body. Her legs were long but not too thin. He could see the muscles working in her thighs as she stepped to the bed.

"What are you looking at?" she asked.

"True beauty."

"Men are always looking at me."

"Any man who didn't wouldn't be normal."

"I just wish they could see what's inside, not just the skin, you know. I'd like a man to see the whole me, the entire package, not just what I look like."

"I'll try my best."

"You already see some of it, don't you?"

"Yeah. And I like it."

"Men have always used me. Or abused me. One or the other. Like Wilson was going to do, leaving me behind. Are you going to do that?"

"I'll treat you right."

"That's easy to say."

"I mean it."

"Just because I'm standing here butt-naked."

"No, I will. I'll take care of you."

"I don't want to be taken care of. I want to be just like you, with you a part of me, me a part of you."

"You already are," Hutto said. "You're as equal as people get."

She sat on the bed and kissed him, then started unbuttoning his shirt.

"I guess you're tired," she said.

"Not yet."

"I guess you want to drop right off to sleep."

"No way."

She slipped off the bed onto her knees and slowly removed his pants.

"Maybe you are ready for a little workout," she

said. "It sure looks that way."

Then she got up and walked to the light switch.

"Leave it on," he said. "I want to look at you."

"I'm worth looking at, huh?"

She left the light on and came back to bed.

"I want to see you, too," she said, and started her workout.

## Chapter Twenty

It was still dark when Hutto woke. He couldn't hear a thing but the steady huffing of Elizabeth's breath. She lay on her side, facing him, naked. The sheet was twisted down around her ankles. He eased from the bed and checked his watch. Four o'clock.

Chico was already up, sitting at the little kitchen table, drinking water from a jelly jar glass. He looked blurred around the edges. Hutto wondered if he'd slept at all.

"Time to roll," Hutto said.

"One last time."

"Let's hope so."

Hutto found a pack of peanut butter crackers, filled a glass with tap water, and joined him.

"Sometimes I have premonitions," Chico said. "And sometimes thoughts of things that came before. It seems I may have lived several lives. Reincarnation is a ridiculous idea, but I can't avoid it. I dreamed I was a soldier. A Roman soldier, perhaps, clanking around in all that iron and leather, or maybe a trooper with King David or Solomon, someone like that. I was killed in battle. I could feel the sword slicing through my gut, and then a dagger cutting my throat in two. I drowned in my own blood. Not a pleasant death."

"None are."

"Each life I dream about always has a death, some by disease, others violent and bloody."

"A death would be the major event in any life, the thing you'd be likely to recall."

"You don't ridicule me for saying these things?"

"I don't know what's right and what's wrong. Maybe reincarnation is possible. Floating around space in a spirit form waiting to come back to earth is possible, maybe. Ghosts are possible. So is ESP. So, no, I'm not saying you're crazy. All I know is you're preoccupied with death. Causing it, living it, toying with it."

"And avoiding it," Chico said. "Most important of all."

"Did you have a premonition about today?"

"No. Just thoughts of past lives."

"And that told you nothing about today?"

"Just to be careful."

"I could have told you that much."

Chico poked around the refrigerator looking for something to eat. He didn't find much, just the things Hutto and Elizabeth had gathered over the past three days.

"No coffee. No eggs. No meat," he said.

"Just wait until tonight. Plenty of everything then."

They sat at the table in the dim light, eating crackers. Neither spoke for a long time. Hutto wondered if Chico was more concerned with what was going on in the Tennessee mountains or back in Colombia.

"Don't tell me you went through this agonizing every time you went on a mission for the Cowboys," he said.

"No, then things were certain. Absolute. An individual needed to be killed. I planned it. No errors were possible. And I did it. It was simple. Clean."

"Fun."

"Not fun at all. But definite. This is indefinite. I don't know what we're doing. You haven't confided in me. Maybe you plan to kill me today, or leave me behind, or any number of things. Can't you see that I'm putting my life in your hands? Whatever we do, today we cut the cord and run, and run some more. Things will never be the same."

"Running beats what we've been doing."

Chico played with a salt shaker, trying to stand it on its side in a little pile of salt.

"This plan of yours, whatever it is, you say it can't fail?"

"You know what they say about the best-laid

plans."

Hutto considered Chico. They needed him as long as he stayed strong. If this little crisis in the hills had whipped him, they'd be better off without him. Hutto was sure some muscle would help, tomorrow or later. Chico would have to get a cut of the money, but a fellow can spend just so much in one lifetime, anyway.

So he told Chico the plan. Chico thought it might work. He'd have done it differently, naturally, but he had more experience with these things, unraveling escape schemes put together by all sorts of people. They always had a flaw.

"Family usually does them in," he said. "They set up a new identity, but always want to go back to see mama. Then a brother, a sister, a wife, a cousin—somebody who is jealous or maybe got kicked around in the past—will tell on them. Anything to get even. Maybe I can believe that *you* are willing to cut out your past entirely, never again see your loved ones, if you have any. But Elizabeth? What if she wants to see papa one more time, or an old boyfriend?"

"What if I try to find my child that's adopted and long gone?" Elizabeth said. She stood in the doorway leading to the hall, propping a shoulder against the frame. Wearing her jeans and by now familiar shirt, she looked ready to go.

"And what about it?"

"I'd love to see him."

"Exactly," Chico said, tapping the salt shaker.

"But I can't. I won't. He doesn't even know me. I don't think I could find him if I had to. You know, like if there was some inherited disease he ought to know about."

"If you try, that's the end of you," Chico said.

"Threatening me?"

"Not me. Whoever takes my place with Ricky Guzman would find the boy and then you. Maybe you both would die."

"Chico, I'm tired of you," she said.

"I should stick to talking about Shakespeare."

"Please, just shut up."

"What about you, Chico?" Hutto said. "You're just the type of guy who would try to sneak back to Baranquilla to see your old mother, right under their noses, just to see if you could do it."

Chico just grunted and shook his head.

"So the past is dead for all of us," Hutto said. "All those people are gone. None of it exists any more."

"I'm a runaway. I've been running for years," Elizabeth said. "It's what I do."

"Until now," Hutto said. She sat down beside him and put her hand on his, not smiling, just watching him. Chico shifted in his chair and excused himself. He wanted to see the cocaine and left them alone for a few minutes.

It was good stuff, he said when he sat down again. He didn't use it himself, but he knew quality. Hutto told him he didn't use it, either. Chico acted like he didn't believe that.

"I thought I was the only one in the business who turned it down," he said.

"I guess you could run a liquor distillery and be a teetotaler," Hutto said. "I'm that way myself."

"We're an unusual pair."

"Weird, I'd say."

"Think of all the morals you've corrupted."

"And the people you've killed."

"We've sent a lot of people to hell, you and me."

"Through hell, to hell. I guess so."

"Isn't being an outlaw just wonderful?" Chico said, rising again and going to the couch. Hutto went outside on the deck, listening to the night noises. After a while, Elizabeth came out wearing a big towel. Its bulk swallowed her up, showing less skin than a lot of dresses, but the sight of her still stirred Hutto.

"I had to take a shower. I can at least be clean, even if I don't have clothes. I didn't come prepared for a long stay," she said.

"You can buy a whole new wardrobe tomorrow."

She put both arms around him, pulling him tight. "You've moved right in on me, haven't you?" she said.

"I've been wondering what you're going to do with yourself the next sixty or seventy years."

"Just get along."

"People are going to be after you when word of this gets around. You know that?"

"I'll make it."

"How? You wouldn't make it past Knoxville. They might find your body in the Tennessee River, if it floats to the top. It might just bump along the bottom, feeding the catfish."

"You can sure break a romantic mood."

"You've got to listen. It could happen."

"I nearly jumped off the bridge into the river once," she said. "But I stopped, because I thought it might not kill me, just hurt real bad."

"A public death is the very worst kind," Chico said, standing behind them at the door. "Just the thing for egotists. If you're serious, get in the bedroom with a pistol. No mistakes, no pain. The job is done. This thing of jumping from a bridge is too much a show."

"Do you always eavesdrop?" she said.

"Miss Elizabeth, angel in a towel, let me say one thing, please," Chico said. "From now on, you and Hutto and I are a trio. Inseparable. Entwined. We will have money to do whatever we want, where we want, but we must do it together, for our own protection. Perhaps not in the same house or even the same town, but always together, as a team. Hutto and I both think this is the only way."

"You're just afraid I'd talk," she said.

"Flesh is weak."

"So where are we going, anyway, if the past is dead for us?"

"Switzerland," Hutto said.

"I don't know Switzerland from baked beans," she said, pulling the towel a little tighter around her, and stepping inside, somehow managing not to touch Chico at all.

## Chapter Twenty-one

Switzerland was a fine place, Chico said, starting to tell her about its beauty, culture, and restaurants.

"I don't care," she said.

"I already have bank accounts there," Hutto said. "I own a house there. I've been getting ready for this several years and didn't even realize it."

"Fine," she said. "I don't care. That's what I told you. As long as you're there, anyplace is okay with me. It's just sort of a shock all at once. Maybe not for you two, but I'm not used to sitting on top of enough coke to supply the universe, while a lot of crazy people are trying to kill me. I just don't want to get left."

Hutto reached out and touched her cheek. "I can leave the past," he said. "I can't leave the future, and you're the future."

She sat at the table, eating a pack of peanut butter crackers, while Hutto and Chico moved the stuff to the Jeep. The coke seemed heavier each time Hutto picked it up. This is the last day, the last time, and he'd never touch the stuff again, he thought.

The stores were still closed when they cut through Gatlinburg, heading back toward Pigeon Forge. Elizabeth followed in the Chevy. Looking in the rearview mirror, Hutto saw she was impatient to speed up, banging her hands on the steering wheel. These young women today, he thought, always hell-bent. But he stuck to the speed limit.

Maybe five miles from Pigeon Forge was Sevierville, the little town that claimed country singer Dolly Parton for a native. They passed Dolly Parton Boulevard and turned right by the Church of God orphanage. A little way out of town, Hutto pulled off the road at a cluttered huddle of buildings. Some private planes were parked there, mostly cheap stuff, but with a few Beeches and Comanches. Beyond them was a runway, paved and surprisingly long for mountain country.

Hutto walked back to the Chevy.

"You know what to do?" he asked.

"I know what you told me."

"You got the pistol?"

"Right here. Wish I knew what to do with it."

"Whatever you did last night to the guy with the Hard Rock Cafe T-shirt was just fine. All you have to do is point it if you get into trouble, then people get wonderfully cooperative."

"What if these people here get nosy?"

"They won't. Just tell them you're waiting for me. They know me. They're used to me."

"Lucky them."

"Righto."

He didn't like leaving her alone, but there was no choice. Chico didn't approve, either. But right now Hutto didn't care what Chico thought.

"This plan has too many weak points," Chico said, looking at Elizabeth sitting in his rented Chevy. "I prefer something watertight."

"Well, we sprung a leak when Wilson took his dive."

"That would have been a good time to quit."

"By then it was too late."

She was working on her makeup in the rearview mirror as they drove off. By the time they got back to the park, the sky was getting lighter. They came to Elkmont, turned left onto the road leading to the campground there, and went past the old Wonderland Hotel. This was one of Hutto's favorite areas in the park. If you had to be around people, this was the way to do it, he thought. It hadn't always been this way. He was sure he'd have hated it back in the old days.

Back in 1901, the Little River Lumber Company came in here and built a mill. By the time they quit cutting, in 1938, they had logged out a half-billion board feet of timber from Elkmont and its neighboring watershed, Tremont.

The Wonderland Hotel offered simple rooms

and simple food, with a beautifully regrown forest, to the lucky few who managed to get a reservation. Further up the road was the Appalachian Club, a summer colony of sorts. The homes here were called cabins, but some would house a half-dozen families in New York City. They were rustic, made of logs and rough boards. One, with designs cut into the shutters, reminded Hutto of a home you might see in Switzerland, maybe somewhere along the Simmental River.

Wealthy people from Knoxville built these places back in the old days, when they arrived here on special trains chugging uphill from town, and spent the summer. Nobody seemed to do that anymore, but it still got crowded in midsummer. When the park was established, the colony somehow managed to get a grandfather clause in the lease. In about ten years that would expire. Then bulldozers might mow down the cabins, so something more natural could spring up. Hutto, who hated developing the mountains, wasn't sure he liked that idea. Somehow the little ragtag colony looked natural, sitting alongside its creek, rotting away amidst the moss and ferns.

Hutto drove across the bridge spanning the narrow Little River, then turned left onto the gravel and dirt road running along its bank. The road stopped about a mile up, blocked by a thick iron bar-gate. Three cars were parked there, pushed in among the trees at the roadside. He and Chico looked them over. A Toyota with Ohio plates, an old Mustang with Nashville plates, and a Ford minivan from Knoxville. Nothing inside but the residue of discarded camping gear, the sort of stuff you think you need but get rid of before you actually start carrying it on your back.

They loaded up the big packs and put them on. The road continued past the bar-gate so hikers could easily pass through. It had been built years before by the loggers and ran straight, with a gradual grade upward. The park service called it the Little River Trail, but it was anything but a trail. Hutto figured even bourbon-swilling, ravioli-chomping Italian mobsters could make it up this road. They hated the Colombians so much they'd walk to hell and back just to beat them out of a few pennies.

It was a mile and four-tenths to the spot where Hutto was headed. In the early morning darkness, it seemed further. But it wasn't a bad hike, even carrying seventy pounds on your back, plus the weight of the weapons. At that point, the Cucumber Gap trail joined Little River, leading off from the right. The river itself was a few yards to the left, roaring over rocks worn smooth during the past few million years.

"Why here?" Chico asked.

"Because they can *get* here easy enough, but they can't hide. We can see the trail a long way, and there are plenty of places to hide and watch.

Plus, it's far enough back to the parking area that we can get a good head start."

"There are too many ways to get ambushed."

"But they don't know where we're going."

"I thought you were in the army. Green Beret or something?"

"Something. What about it?"

"Good thing you weren't a general. Battle plans like this, and you'd have been dead a long a time ago."

"Maybe that was our trouble in Vietnam."

They hid the stuff in a natural depression beneath some rhododendron along the river. It took four trips back and forth to get all the coke there, so by the time the sun crept over the treetops on the ridge to the east, they'd hiked over ten miles carrying a mountain of it. Even Chico was tired. He reclined on a smooth rock at the water's edge. Hutto thought he was asleep until he whirled and nearly gunned down a squirrel working over a nut further down the bank.

The sun made the river gorge glow with light. The rapids around the rocks sparkled. Butterflies began going about their business, darting around, settling on the little purple flowers growing everywhere.

Hutto left Chico there, dabbling well away from the cocaine. He walked out of the rhododendron thicket and stopped, looking everything over. Couldn't see a thing, he thought. Nothing in there but rabbits and mice. You'd never guess there was a wildman Colombian killer lurking around, with enough pistol power to hold off the Mexican army.

Walking out made him feel good. It was the first time he'd been alone in several days. Being alone gave him time to think, and he liked that. He'd hated crowds ever since he'd pulled that two-year prison vacation.

Going without the backpack made him feel light and bouncy. This would be a good trail to run sometime, he thought, and then remembered that, with luck, he'd never see it again. He'd be gone forever, one way or the other, and the Smokies would have to grow older without him.

## Chapter Twenty-two

He drove the Jeep back to the Wonderland Hotel, parked, walked onto the wide plank porch, and sat in a straight-backed rocking chair. A couple of other people were already out stirring, but nobody thought it strange that he was there. For all they knew, he could have been a guest, or meeting someone.

Rocking, with one foot on the porch railing, he looked at home. People came by, nodding, commenting on the quality of their breakfast, or the fairness of the weather, or speculating about whether they'd spot a bear that day. The hotel employees loved to talk about bears coming in after food and garbage, sometimes even climbing the outside stairs.

Nine o'clock came and went. Nobody showed. Plans, he thought. Maybe Chico was right. Maybe a five-year-old could have planned it better. Without Wilson, things had been different. He'd tried to compensate, but maybe he'd been wrong. Who could say?

Nine-thirty. Still nobody came. Hutto began to worry. Anything could have gone wrong. The plane could have crashed. They could have had a wreck. One of them could have had a heart attack, or the whole lot of them could be fighting over something, a girl, maybe. You just can't rely on people, Hutto thought. You can't trust them, even when they're honest. And when they're dishonest, it's a whole new ball game.

At ten o'clock, a new black Eldorado pulled into the parking lot. Three dark-haired men got out, looking like they'd just gotten a shipment of hiking gear from the L.L. Bean catalog. You couldn't tell them apart from the Colombians, Hutto decided. These folks ought to wear different-colored jerseys, with numbers, so you can tell who's who.

They walked single file onto the porch, each shuffling along in his own way, carrying himself in that unmistakable tough-guy manner. The really good ones, the ones that stay alive — like Chico — don't walk that way, Hutto thought. They look just like everybody else, or like everybody else wants to look like. That avoids trouble.

These guys were looking for trouble.

Hutto took a deep breath, dropped his feet off the railing, stood up, and said, "You're late."

"Well, you know, it was a hard night, and all that."

The man who spoke looked smart enough to be in charge, maybe smart enough to move up in the organization. Hutto figured he was a junior executive. They wouldn't send a dummy out on this kind of deal. A smart guy smelling out trouble. That was just what Hutto didn't need.

"You've taken care of your end of it?" Hutto asked.

"We always do."

"I don't know a thing about you."

"Business is business. No big thing."

"Let's see."

Hutto led them inside to the telephone near the registration desk. The clerk checked them over.

"We're booked for tonight," he said.

"We're just here to eat," Hutto told him.

He plugged a quarter into the phone and dialed a number. It rang four times before Elizabeth picked it up.

"Yes?" she said.

"Is everything there?"

"The plane's here," she said.

"What about the cargo?"

"It, too. I counted it the way you said, and it looks about right."

"You're sure?"

"I guess."

"You don't sound very sure."

"I'm doing my best."

"And the pilot?"

"Two guys flew in and another guy in a big black car picked them up and they drove off together."

"So you're ready on your end?"

"Let's get it over with," she said.

He hung up and turned to the three men watching him. "Why don't we get in a short hike before we eat," he said. "Just something to get your blood going."

They walked to the Eldorado. The two silent ones got in front. He and the talker rode in back. He told them where to go. The talker explained how if anything happened to them, Hutto would never get the plane out of Sevierville.

"How will you do that? I mean if something happens to you?"

"We're always prepared."

"Then you'd better be a good boy, so I don't have to get nasty with you," Hutto said.

"A funny fellow."

"Somebody else said something like that to me not long ago."

"So?"

"He's dead now."

The talker cracked his window and lit a cigarette with a gold lighter. "You know, the boss wants to drive these Spics out of business. That's how come he'll deal with scum like you. But you know what? You take me, I'm different. I can't stand doublecrosses, even when it's the Spics you cross. Guys like that ought to be hung up by their thumbs, let the ants eat their eyeballs," he said.

"My, my, I'd better watch out," Hutto said.

"Now, me, I make my living legitimate. I'm straight."

"Just pure old-fashioned crime. No funny stuff, right?"

"Damn right."

"Mister Clean, too."

"I don't like this drug business. The broads and the gambling, a few rackets, that's enough for me."

"Too many weirdos in the drug business," Hutto said.

"You said it."

They crossed the bridge and turned onto the dirt road, passing the house that looked like it belonged in Switzerland. Down the gravel road, the parking area had just about filled up. They managed to squeeze the Eldorado in between two trees, and got out.

"You never heard of hotel rooms, say, like the Hyatt or the Marriott? Looks like half the world is out here, for Christ's sake," the talker said.

"I like doing business out in the open. I've got nothing to hide."

"Yeah, well, we do."

"Like what?"

"Like our faces, that's what."

They put on packs and took a drink from their

water bottles. "You don't really need those guns," Hutto said. "You could take them out of the packs and leave them here. It'd be a lot lighter."

"There might be animals in the woods. We'd have to protect ourselves."

So they set off up the old logging road. Hutto led the way. First, there's the hillbilly army out to get me, he thought. Then, the Colombian army. And now the Italian army. And what army after this? Maybe none. Maybe. Maybe the war is over after this battle.

Even the talker was quiet, so Hutto didn't have to deal with them as they plodded along. These guys weren't exactly what Hutto had expected. He imagined some short round guys showing up chewing cigars. These three were in shape, the kind of fitness you get hanging out at a health club, riding stationary bikes and playing tennis. They looked like they'd never hiked before.

They were slow, lagging behind. Hutto wondered if they were playing a trick, then decided they just didn't know how to walk properly. Too many Cadillacs had hauled them too many places. It took half an hour to get to where the Cucumber Gap trail branched off.

Chico was well hidden, wherever he was. Hutto looked and couldn't see a trace of him. The stuff was right where it was when he'd left, on the river bank, hidden under the rhododendron. The talker's companions got on their knees and counted the packages, checking occasionally to see if they were really filled with cocaine and not sugar or flour or something worthless.

"It's here," the talker said when they finished.

"You expected a trick?"

"There's always a trick."

"You've done this before, then."

"We're not beginners."

"Neither am I."

"So where's the trick?"

"Right here," came a voice from the river. The talker turned to see Chico rising from a pile of rocks on the bank where he'd been hiding.

"A Spic," the talker said. "I might have known there'd be a Spic in on it."

"Please, no ethnic slurs," Chico said. He balanced a big pistol in his right hand, stroking the underside of the barrel with his left, as though it were a precious, valued, and loved thing.

"I'm sure you think you can take our money and keep the dope yourself. Double your profits," the talker said.

"Maybe that's what you'd do, but there's only so much money I can spend in one lifetime," Hutto said. "I figure this is about my limit. Doubling it wouldn't do me any good."

"Then what's the Spic here for?"

"The gentleman is here for insurance purposes. He insures that I get away from here."

"Unfortunately, I must ask you to stay," the

talker said. Then he looked up through the brush toward the trail. "Stevie," he said. "Are you here?"

Then a guy, an inch or two shy of seven feet tall and a few pounds past three hundred, stepped into view. He smiled, showing crooked teeth yellowed from smoking. He was holding a pistol with a silencer.

For some reason, men holding guns always expected their prey to dive to their right, so Hutto dove left, reached down his leg, and whipped out his knife. In one motion he sent it flying to Stevie's heart. The big man tumbled down some rocks and his pistol rattled beside him, hot from the shot that just missed Hutto.

One of the two quiet ones started moving about the time Hutto did, going for a pistol in his pack lying on the ground. As he reached it, Chico shot him through the chest. He flopped onto the pile of cocaine, blood staining the brown packages.

The other quiet one was darting for Chico by then and slammed him to the rocks, knocking the pistol away. He whipped out a wire garrote and wrapped it around the Colombian's neck. There was nothing Chico could do but squeeze his fingers between the wire and his soft skin. The wire instantly sliced the fingers, spurting blood everywhere.

The talker and Hutto dove for Chico's gun at the same time, bumping heads. Hutto drove the heel of his right hand hard into the talker's forehead, popping him between the eyes. He rolled back, and Hutto came up with the weapon, lowered it steadily at Chico and his assailant as they struggled on the rocks, and fired. The Italian slumped across Chico's back, bleeding from the spot where the part in his hair started, minus the back of his head.

By then the talker was going for Stevie's gun, but Hutto flipped around and stopped him.

"Now what would you do that for?" Hutto said. His ears were ringing and he had a hard time hearing his own voice. "Come over here and have a seat."

The talker sat down on a rock by the river. He crossed his fingers, working his hands back and forth. "Let's think about this," he said.

"Shut up," Hutto said. He went over to look at Chico. He was still lying there with the dead man on his back. Hutto rolled the guy off and carefully unwrapped the garrote from Chico's fingers. Two were cut to the bone, but he'd managed to save his neck from any real damage.

"Are you all right?" Hutto asked.

"All right but mad as hell. Nobody does that to me," Chico muttered.

"They did."

"Perhaps it really is time to retire."

"That's what I've been telling you."

Chico crawled over to the river and soaked his fingers in the cool water. Then he took off his shirt and began washing out the blood. The talker sat on the rock watching this silently.

"May I speak?" he finally said.

"I figured you would," Hutto said.

"I would like to say that I am just the messenger. I have my orders. I'm a good soldier. I carry them out."

"So what?"

"So, it was my boss who ordered you killed. He couldn't give up that much money. We've been having hard times lately."

"Well, now the payroll is considerably less," Hutto said.

"You were honest with us," the talker said. "I regretted having to do it."

"Especially now."

"We're just little people here, you and I. I was doing my job. What we think or don't think, doesn't matter."

"Yes, it does."

"It's nice to think so."

The talker started to get up from his rock. Hutto pointed the pistol at him and he sat back down. Then Hutto walked over and picked up Stevie's pistol.

"Where'd you get the big guy, anyway?" he asked.

"Stevie was too dumb for college basketball and too slow for the pros," the talker said. "He needed a job."

The talker began working industriously at some dirt lodged in his fingernails. Chico was through with his washing and stood bare-chested beside Hutto. His bleeding had slowed down. His hair, normally neatly combed, looked wild.

"I'll take care of this guy," he told Hutto.

"Wait, I think you need me. I know things that might get you out alive," the talker said.

"We're doing pretty good so far," Hutto said.

"You don't know what you need to know. I'll help. There's a trap. We've got guys waiting for you. I can call them off. I won't even ask for a cut of the money, or any coke."

"That's kind of you," Chico said.

"You don't know anything," the talker said. "You'll never make it out of here. And even if you do, my boss will be hot for revenge. You won't go far."

"We'll risk it," Hutto said.

"You'll lose your lives and your money."

"If we let you go, we'll certainly lose," Chico said.

"I don't understand you guys. What are you going to do, talk us to death?" Hutto said.

"You have the guns."

"I thought you Italians at least had a sense of honor."

"Too much money, huh?"

"Nobody can handle the idea of that much money."

"So why did you bring the money on the plane?"

"To make it look proper. We knew you'd check it."

"No, the reason you brought real money was because you were going to take it and disappear yourself," Hutto said.

"You've gone crazy," the Italian said.

"I know you. I can read your mind. We all have our special little talents, and that's mine."

The talker turned around to watch the river flow. He tossed a few stones into it, then some leaves, following their swirl downstream. His body folded into a tight little bundle on the rock.

"Kill me, then," he said. "Just kill me now."

He spun on the rock to face them. Chico took Stevie's pistol from Hutto, checking the silencer—ever the professional—making sure there were bullets in the clip. He held it lightly in one hand, weighing it, considering its potential.

"Beg for your life?" Chico asked the talker.

"No, thank you."

Chico turned to Hutto, looking him in the eye. "This is how you do it. No discussion. Professionally," he said.

"Whatever you say," Hutto said.

Chico nodded. "How do you want it?" he asked the talker.

The man pointed to the center of his forehead, just above the spot where his eyebrows met. He stared at Chico and a little smile curled his lips upward.

"My pleasure," Chico said.

He drew the pistol level, held it steady, aimed, pulled the trigger, and a round dot filled with blood exactly where the man had pointed. When he fell, Hutto saw the back of his head had blown away.

Then Chico walked to the other three and pumped a bullet apiece into their heads.

Hutto slumped down against a rock. "I'll have to hand it to these guys," he said. "At least they didn't pussyfoot around. They came out here to kill us and, by God, that's what they tried to do. No psychology. No games. Why did you ask him where he wanted it, anyway?"

"Courtesy. The choice is good."

"Choice of how to die?"

Chico nodded. "I let him choose his death."

"What if he'd wanted to wrestle you for it or something crazy?"

"I don't have to grant the request. I would shoot him there, anyway. At least he dies thinking it was his decision. Something about that seems right."

"I'll have to remember that next time," Hutto said.

"Let's hope there is no next time."

"Amen to that."

"I think we still have something to do," Chico said.

"What's that?"

"Well, this is your cocaine. You can do whatever you want with it. It's safe to say you can't sell to the Italians now. You can't deal with Ricky Guzman. I suppose that brings it down to the blacks, Chicanos, the outlaw bikers, perhaps. Maybe the Chinese or the Vietnamese, though they're difficult to deal with. Of course, they wouldn't have the money, not like the big guys do."

"Who needs money?" Hutto said. "It's not worth all this."

"How many people died for this cocaine?"

"Let's see. Fourteen I know of right offhand."

"Fourteen too many."

"Yes."

"And it will just continue, this chain of death. The big guys will kill the little guys, or vice versa. Then the dealers will kill each other, not many, but surely two or three more will die. And then on the street, how many? How many children will stuff this up their noses or smoke it and have a private hell?"

"You're too much, Chico."

"It's my job, being too much."

"But what you say is true."

Hutto crawled on his knees to the pile of cocaine near the talker's body. He pulled a brown paper-wrapped kilo out and felt its heft. His knife made a soft slitting sound slicing into it. When he turned it over, the powder fell into the water of

Little River and disappeared, rushing over the rocks, heading downstream, moving into the Tennessee River, and from there into the Ohio, and then the Mississippi. From there, it would ride the currents of the Gulf of Mexico, a molecule or two making it back to Colombia.

"Such a little thing that goes so fast makes men crazy," Chico said, watching. Then he got on his knees and helped.

It took half an hour to dump it all in the river. Hutto was fascinated by how easy it was to get rid of the stuff after all the trouble it had caused. He felt like a kid doing something slightly naughty, and the thought of all that potential money just disappearing made him a little giddy. He started laughing as he sliced and dumped, and then Chico began to laugh, too, moving in rhythm with him, realizing the two of them were doing something no one had ever done before, or would ever do again.

They gathered the paper and stuffed it into their backpacks, but left the four bodies lying where they were. There were too many rocks to bury them where they fell and too many people on this trail to risk carrying them anywhere else. By the time they began to smell and somebody found them, Hutto and Chico would be a few thousand miles away.

They hurried down the trail, passing a young family on the way. The woman wore hiking shorts and the man was explaining to two little girls, about ten years old, how the mountains came to be, how ancient they were.

Hutto and Chico went around the bar-gate and ignored the black Eldorado. This meant they had to walk a couple of miles more to get to the Jeep parked at the Wonderland Hotel, which was fine with Hutto because he planned to never ride in another black Cadillac. Chico said it was a fine day for a walk in the woods along a roaring river. Hutto knew Chico was in pain. His hand was clotting blood. It needed stitches, but wouldn't get any, not for a while, anyway.

"How you feeling?" he asked.

"It'll go away," Chico told him. "Everything goes away if you give it time."

## Chapter Twenty-three

The Jeep waited. They turned it around in the gravel and dirt Wonderland Hotel parking lot, and started down the winding lane heading back to the paved park road. Hutto had decided the Italians were bluffing, that there was no trap, no ambush. Stevie, the giant, must have been hiding in their trunk all along. The logical time to get them was on the way back to their hotel, and they didn't see a thing but some hikers and a group of children playing in the campground.

Then a black Eldorado pulled out from a service road in front of them. The driver blocked their path and looked at them a long couple of seconds. Hutto stopped the Jeep, trying to figure this new move. Then the window lowered on the Eldorado's passenger side and a guy pointed a pistol and fired at them. The shot poked through the Jeep's windshield and starred the glass. Hutto threw the Jeep into reverse and backed up the lane.

The Eldorado zoomed around and down to the main road. It squealed its tires and sped away. Hutto let the Jeep ease forward slowly.

"Must be Stevie's car," he said. "They had to meet the other guys here. Drove up from Atlanta or something."

"They're scared," Chico said.

"They're more than scared. They're heading to the airport."

Hutto spun the Jeep onto the pavement and started tracking the Eldorado. The gears whined as he pushed it to catch up.

"Elizabeth doesn't have a chance with these guys," Chico said.

"You're a comforting guy to have along. Always cheerful."

The trees and rocks went by in a blur as they got up to speed. The river and road moved from Elkmont together, fraternal twins, one asphalt, the other water and rock, pushing through soil and trees and more rock. As a child, Hutto used to swim in the river, further down at a place called the Sinks, and further will at another spot called the Townsend Y. Hutto saw a fisherman, standing knee-deep in water, drop a fancy fly onto the swirl and follow it past a little pool where the river briefly calmed before dashing on its way. There were always lots of fishermen here—usually with Ohio or Michigan plates on their campers—but few fish.

The residue from the stuff they'd dumped in the river should be this far by now. Hutto wondered how it might affect the flora and fauna. The wildlife might get even wilder. Maybe it wouldn't change or kill things. After all, it was a natural substance. But so was the flu, and the plague.

Chico rode quietly for a while, watching the black car swerving in front of them. Then he stirred a little and spoke. "I thought I had killed my last man," he said.

"You can't haul your guns off to a pawnshop just yet," Hutto said.

"After this, I'll never fire another weapon. I plan to devote my life to doing good. Sounds pompous, but that's what I want."

"Sometimes the only good comes from the barrel of a gun, Chico."

"Killing is not a good thing, Hutto. God gives life. He should be the one to take it, not me."

"Maybe you're the instrument of God, after all."

The Jeep had now pushed to within fifty yards of the Eldorado. The driver kept looking back at them in the rearview mirror, losing time, making it hard to stay on the road.

"If God wants someone dead, he can make them drive off a cliff or something. He doesn't need me to do his dirty work," Chico said.

"Don't retire just yet."

Hutto had the Jeep up to ninety, whipping along a road built to handle forty-five-mile-per-hour traffic. The Eldorado driver didn't know the road and kept running off the pavement in the curves. Hutto wondered what an enforcement ranger might do if one happened across this little race. He didn't really mind killing the guys in the Eldorado if it came to that, but he didn't want to kill a ranger. He didn't think he could do it. Killing a bad guy was one thing. Killing a guy who spent his time catching speeding tourists and handing out fines for camping without a permit, getting paid $14,000 a year, was something else.

The Eldorado came to where the Elkmont road met the Little River road and turned right. Hutto was so close behind it was easy to see the driver's desperate eyes as he checked them out. Up the road a bit, he took a blind curve wide, well over the center line. Hutto followed, staying within his lane, and saw the guy on the passenger side firing his pistol wildly at them. There was no way he could hit them, flailing around like that.

"These guys are a little crazy," Chico said.

"Aren't they all?"

The road went into a series of dips and curves where solid rock hugged the right side and the left dropped off a steep embankment.

Hutto geared the Jeep down, dropping a little off the pace, slowing for the curves. But the Eldorado slammed on, bouncing hard. The passenger stuck his head out the window and over the roof and took another shot at them from the other side of the curve they were in. Then the Eldorado slid too wide, all the way into the opposite lane. A Toyota minivan came the opposite direction, holding hard to its side of the road around the curve. The Italian whipped to the right to avoid it, planted the front of his fancy car in the rock cliff, whirled around across the road, flipped up so the Eldorado caught air, and sailed in a perfect arc to the bottom of a ravine.

The Toyota driver pulled off the road, opened his door, and threw up. His wife and three kids scrambled out of the minivan and watched the spectacle. Hutto slowed the Jeep to a crawl, taking a long look himself.

"That guy was crazy," the woman said to him as he leaned out his window. "Absolutely crazy."

"Our thoughts exactly," he said, and kept driving.

They rode a mile or so before Chico spoke.

"That's sixteen," he said.

"Sixteen what?"

"Sixteen people dead for your cocaine."

"It's not my cocaine."

"Whose is it, then?"

"Let's not quibble. At least we didn't have to shoot them."

"Small comfort."

"Now you can start devoting your life to saving the little children."

"There are worse things."

"I'm going to devote the next hour to getting us out of here alive, and the rest of my life to getting up at sunrise and not wondering if I'm going to be around to see it set," Hutto said.

"We're free now. There's no more Chico, no more Hutto," Chico said.

"If you're not Chico, who are you? What's your name, anyway? Chico is a nickname, right?"

"My name is Rafael Alleman. Chico means Little Boy. I used so many false names, so many fake passports, that having a name like Chico simplified matters."

"Mine is Leonard. Leonard Hutto. Mom's maiden name was Leonard. Never seemed to fit me. That's why I just go by the last name."

"Now you can call yourself whatever you want. Abe Lincoln. Al Capone. You name it."

Three cars full of enforcement rangers passed them going the other direction, back to where the Eldorado committed suicide. Hutto took the bypass around Gatlinburg, eased through Pigeon Forge's stupid thirty-five-miles-per-hour zone, getting one last look at Mystery Mountain, the various outlet malls, Archie Campbell's Hee Haw Village, and the putt-putt golf courses with their cement wild animals, lions and tigers and elephants and dinosaurs. Then Sevierville came up, looking partly old and substantial, partly new and plastic.

Hutto could see that the plastic was beginning

to win out. In five years, Sevierville would have its own crop of dinosaurs and water slides owned by people from Nashville and Little Rock and New York.

Elizabeth waited at the little airport, sitting on the hood of the Chevy. She looked lean and strong and very blonde in the bright sunlight. A big heavy man in a blue jogging suit stood beside her. They weren't talking.

"This guy says he knows you," she said. "I didn't tell him a thing. He knew all about me. Even how much I weigh. He's some kind of strange guy. I tried to run him off, but he wouldn't go."

"Pulled a gun on me, she did," the man said.

"She's really a sweetie, Sully," Hutto said, and shook the big man's hand. "Don't let it bother you. She thought she was doing her job."

"I did it, too," she said and hopped down to the ground.

"Remember when I told you about that guy from Atlanta that was going to get you out of here?" Hutto asked her. "Well, Sully is that guy."

Hutto introduced him. He was Robert Sullivan, a handy guy to know. He worked out of Atlanta and did a big business in false passports and fake identification of all sorts. Give him a couple of days and he could make you over into an entirely new person, with a background, family history, the whole bit.

Before Hutto and Wilson started out this time, they had Sully make them some new, clean ID. It cost them a couple grand each, a bargain any way you look at it. Now Hutto wanted him to fix up something for Elizabeth. He'd done everything he could in Atlanta and agreed to meet them here to finalize it.

"I been trying to do her and she won't let me," he said.

"He wants to take my picture. I thought he was some kind of creep. You mean all along he was trying to make me a passport?"

"I can't come right out and say it," Sully said. "I thought you'd know. You could be the wrong person. Christ's sake."

"Sully, I really appreciate you coming all the way up here, but we're in a big hurry. So if you could just do whatever it is you have to do, so we can get started," Hutto said.

"This one is going to cost you ten big ones," he said. "Wilson's untimely demise has me worried. I don't think they can trace him back to me, but you never know."

"Ten thousand is no problem. Just get it over with."

Sully took Elizabeth inside a deserted hangar, set up a screen behind her, and a camera just like those the quickie photo shops use to shoot passport pictures. It took about five minutes to finish.

"Click, click, and it's over? Ten grand? Boy,

that's two thousand table dances," she said.

"You're paying for my skill and potential danger," Sully said.

"Still, that's good work if you can get it," she said.

"You're an innocent girl," the big man said, packing his gear away in a Ford van.

"Nobody calls me innocent any more."

"And nobody calls you girl, either," Hutto said.

"It's okay," she said.

"You mean, after all that yelling and fussing about it, you don't mind being called a girl?"

"It just doesn't bother me any more."

"Go figure it," Hutto said.

Chico had been checking out the airplane. "It looks ready to go," he said.

"What do you know about airplanes?" Chico asked.

"Not much. Buckle your seat belt before takeoff. Bring your seat backs and tray tables to the full upright and locked positions."

"Then how would you know it's ready?"

"I should say, I'm ready."

"Aren't we all?"

Sully said he was heading back to Atlanta. Hutto rummaged around in the plane and came back with ten thousand dollars. "Nothing personal, Sully, but I hope I never see you again," he said.

"Here's luck to you," the big man said, and

drove away.

Elizabeth stood there with her arms folded across her chest, looking at the crest of the mountains miles past Pigeon Forge and Gatlinburg. That would be Mount Le Conte she was looking at. Kephart, Collins, all those others they'd fought, were hidden.

"We have to talk," she said.

"We can talk in the air. I have a feeling a busload of Colombians is going to pull up here any minute."

"I want to talk while my two feet are firmly on the ground."

"Okay, what do you want to know?"

"Tell me about Switzerland. I want to know where we're going, and how we're going to get there, and what we're going to do when we're there. Chico here says we're all sticking together, but I should have my say, too."

"Ever hear of a place called Brienz?" Hutto asked.

"What do you think?"

"It's a little town on the most beautiful lake I've ever seen. A few miles up the road from Interlaken. Ever hear of that place?"

"No."

"It's sort of a tourist town, kind of like Gatlinburg, but done up better. A lot of Americans go there to ski. It's on a patch of land between the lake that Brienz is on and another lake called the

Thuner See."

"So what's so special about it?"

"Well, Interlaken is nice, but Brienz is just about the best place on earth. You can sit on your porch there and see the Eiger and the Jungfrau and the Schreckhorn. Those mountains make the Smokies look like foothills. Brienz is peaceful. It's quiet. I guess it's slow-paced. But it's still on a main road and Americans are common there. It's not that far to Bern or Luzern. So you can go to the big town, if you want to blow the carbon out sometime."

"And you want to live there."

"Well, I already own a house there. Bought it a few years back after I rolled in a lot of money one time. I thought it might come in handy sometime. Now's the time. They speak mostly German there, but a lot speak English, too. They're friendly people. They like to help you out. There's a little paved walkway along the lake, and in summer you can just sort of hang out there and meet everybody in town. There's even a movie theater where they show American films. You'll like it there."

"No doubt you already have a girlfriend there."

"That's the one thing I'm missing in Brienz."

"It wouldn't be like I was your prisoner?"

"We'd be new people. We could go where we wanted and do what we wanted. We could go down to Aigle and Martigny, where it's like the Mediterranean, or up north to Stein am Rhein, which is a little town on the river that's just like medieval times. We could run over to Gstaad and ski with the other rich folks or to St. Moritz, or do anything."

"Could we go to the big beer bust at that place in Germany?"

"Oktoberfest? In Munich? Whatever you want."

"I might want a lot."

"It's okay. So do I."

"So you're asking me to spend the rest of my life with you?"

"Yes. If you will," he said.

"Then ask."

"I swore I'd never do this again."

"It doesn't pay to swear."

"Well, okay," he said, looking up at the mountains. He felt a little queazy. He hadn't planned on doing this just yet. "Elizabeth, we haven't really known each other all that long, and the past few days have been hectic and not all that pleasant, but I want you to spend the rest of your life with me, sharing everything I have."

"It's a deal," she said.

"I've never heard such babble," Chico said. "And on a dingy little airport runway. Definitely not Romeo and Juliet."

"It's Romeo and Juliet to me," she said. "He may not be Romeo, but he least he didn't come buy me away from some strip joint."

"Pardon me," Chico said.

"I would have," Hutto said.

"Would have what?"

"Gotten you away from that strip joint. If I'd just have known you."

"But then we'd have missed all this excitement," she said. "What I want to know now is how we get from here to Switzerland."

"Ever heard of the Netherlands Antilles?" he asked.

"Here we go again. Twenty questions."

"You've heard of the Bahamas? The Virgin Islands?"

"Wilson was going to take me sometime."

"The Netherlands Antilles are down that way. It's three little islands making up their own little country and it's almost all the way back to Colombia, right where this started. Aruba, Bonair, and Curacao. Officially it's part of the Netherlands, you know, Dutch. Curacao is an interesting place, with windmills and farms and good beaches, but we won't be there long enough to do much. I know some people there who are pretty good money launderers."

"Of course."

"They're going to take care of our money and refuel and feed us. Then we'll fly across the Atlantic to some islands off the coast of Spain."

"Let me guess. You know people there, too."

"It pays to know people."

"I bet. What happens there?"

"We rest up a day or two, then we take a fishing boat to La Coruna, which is a little town on a bay. Then we get a car and drive ourselves to Switzerland."

"Across the borders."

"No problem," Hutto said. "We've got legitimate passports, and our friends in Curacao will already have wired our money to my bank accounts in Switzerland."

"Still, what if there's a problem?"

"We buy them off. Border guards are poorly paid. They'd jump at the chance. Don't worry."

"Too many people see us," Chico said. "Perhaps that is a weak point."

"These are good people, all of them. Plus, none of them know who I really am."

"But they'll see me. Her, too. They'll know something is funny."

"They'll know, but they won't care, because we'll tip them so well."

"Money. The magic ingredient."

"That's how the world works."

"I still think I'll work on my disguises," Chico said.

"Help yourself."

"Let me see my picture," Elizabeth said.

"What picture?"

"In that passport you paid so much money for."

He hadn't wanted her to see it just yet, but he let her have it. Of course, she didn't like the picture. "It doesn't even look like me," she said. "My mouth is all screwed up and I look fat. I'm not that fat, am I?"

"Looks just like you," Chico said.

"Shut up."

"Pardon."

"You mean I'll have to live with this picture forever?"

"At least until we find someone to make a new one."

"Let me see yours," she said to Hutto.

He dug his out and handed it to her.

"Yours is better," she said.

"I think yours looks just fine," Hutto said.

She held them both up, comparing Sully's work against itself.

"These people have the same name," she said. "Wilkinson. I'm Linda Wilkinson and you're Thomas Wilkinson."

"That's the story."

"What's the deal?"

"Well, the deal is, we're married, complete with marriage certificate and everything."

"You're kidding. Aren't you kidding?"

"No, that's the way it is. Sully thought it was best that way."

"Sully thought. He's a matchmaker, then."

"You could say that."

"Now, that's the damndest thing," she said. "One minute I'm standing here as old Elizabeth, a bad girl runaway from Alabama, and the next thing I know I'm a married woman."

"A rich married woman."

"Did he give us any kids?"

"He thought we could take care of that on our own."

"You could have at least asked me if I wanted to be married."

"There wasn't time. I had to make a decision."

"So you didn't even ask."

"I wasn't even sure we'd be alive, much less married."

"Then ask me now."

"I just asked you to spend the rest of your life with me."

"No, you asked Elizabeth. Ask this woman. What's her name? Linda MacDonald Wilkinson. Ask Linda MacDonald of the famous well-to-do MacDonalds from Nashville, Tennessee."

"Okay, Linda MacDonald. I've only known you four days, but I've never met anyone I wanted so much. I thought I was past caring about women. But I'm not. Maybe it never gets out of your system. But I want to marry you. I want to make you an honest woman, Linda MacDonald."

"I do," she said. "I do and I will."

Chico coughed politely. "Could you kiss the bride and let's get moving? That busload of Ricky's boys is probably almost here. Or the police. Or someone even worse."

Then Hutto got them settled into the plane. He left the keys to the Jeep and the Chevy with the guy running the airstrip as payment for his trouble. The plane checked out perfect, engines running without a knock. The gas tanks were full, and they could cruise all day.

The plane lifted off the runway, and Sevierville fell away beneath them, with the plastic and the old brick coming together into a single pattern. Then they were over the mountains, heading southward. Mount Le Conte was so close and huge he wanted to stick a hand out and fondle it. He thought about the bear on its summit and wondered if anyone had found it. The green depths were so thick he couldn't see any trails across it. He knew them all, anyway, every foot of every path, every rock, every waterfall and cliff. Then Mount Kephart rose into view, smaller but still mighty, and Hutto thought again of Horace Kephart and how he had to leave everything behind to find his purpose in life. He'd left a family and job, everything. All Hutto was leaving was Hutto.

Hutto couldn't look away from the mountains below, so he just set the airplane's nose on course and gazed at them one last time, taking in their power, their beauty, remembering how ancient they were, thinking of earthquakes and seas and fires and all the storms heaven and hell could offer, and still these hills endured, changing grain by grain, but always enduring.

He watched them pass beneath his craft and then away behind them until they were gone. Good-bye to all that, he thought. Good-bye to all that.

## ESPIONAGE FICTION BY LEWIS PERDUE

**THE LINZ TESTAMENT** (17-117, $4.50)
Throughout World War Two the Nazis used awesome power to silence the Catholic Church to the atrocities of Hitler's regime. Now, four decades later, its existence has brought about the most devastating covert war in history — as a secret battle rages for possession of an ancient relic that could shatter the foundations of Western religion: The Shroud of Veronica, irrefutable evidence of a second Messiah. For Derek Steele it is a time of incomprehensible horror, as the ex-cop's relentless search for his missing wife ensnares him in a deadly international web of KGB assassins, Libyan terrorists, and bloodthirsty religious zealots.

**THE DA VINCI LEGACY** (17-118, $4.50)
A fanatical sect of heretical monks fired by an ancient religious hatred. A page from an ancient manuscript which could tip the balance of world power towards whoever possesses it. And one man, caught in a swirling vortex of death and betrayal, who alone can prevent the enslavement of the world by the unholy alliance of the Select Brothers and the Bremen Legation. The chase is on — and the world faces the horror of The Da Vinci Legacy.

**QUEENS GATE RECKONING** (17-164, $3.95)
Qaddafi's hit-man is the deadly emissary of a massive and cynical conspiracy with origins far beyond the Libyan desert, in the labyrinthine bowels of the Politburo . . . and the marble chambers of a seditious U.S. Government official. And rushing headlong against this vast consortium of treason is an improbable couple — a wounded CIA operative and defecting Soviet ballerina. Together they hurtle toward the hour of ultimate international reckoning.

*Available wherever paperbacks are sold, or order direct from the Publisher. Send cover price plus 50¢ per copy for mailing and handling to Pinnacle Books, Dept.17-264, 475 Park Avenue South, New York, N.Y. 10016. Residents of New York, New Jersey and Pennsylvania must include sales tax. DO NOT SEND CASH.*